BEAUTY AND THE ALPHA BEAST

WOLF SHIFTER FAIRY TALE RETELLINGS
BOOK ONE

BELLA MOONDRAGON

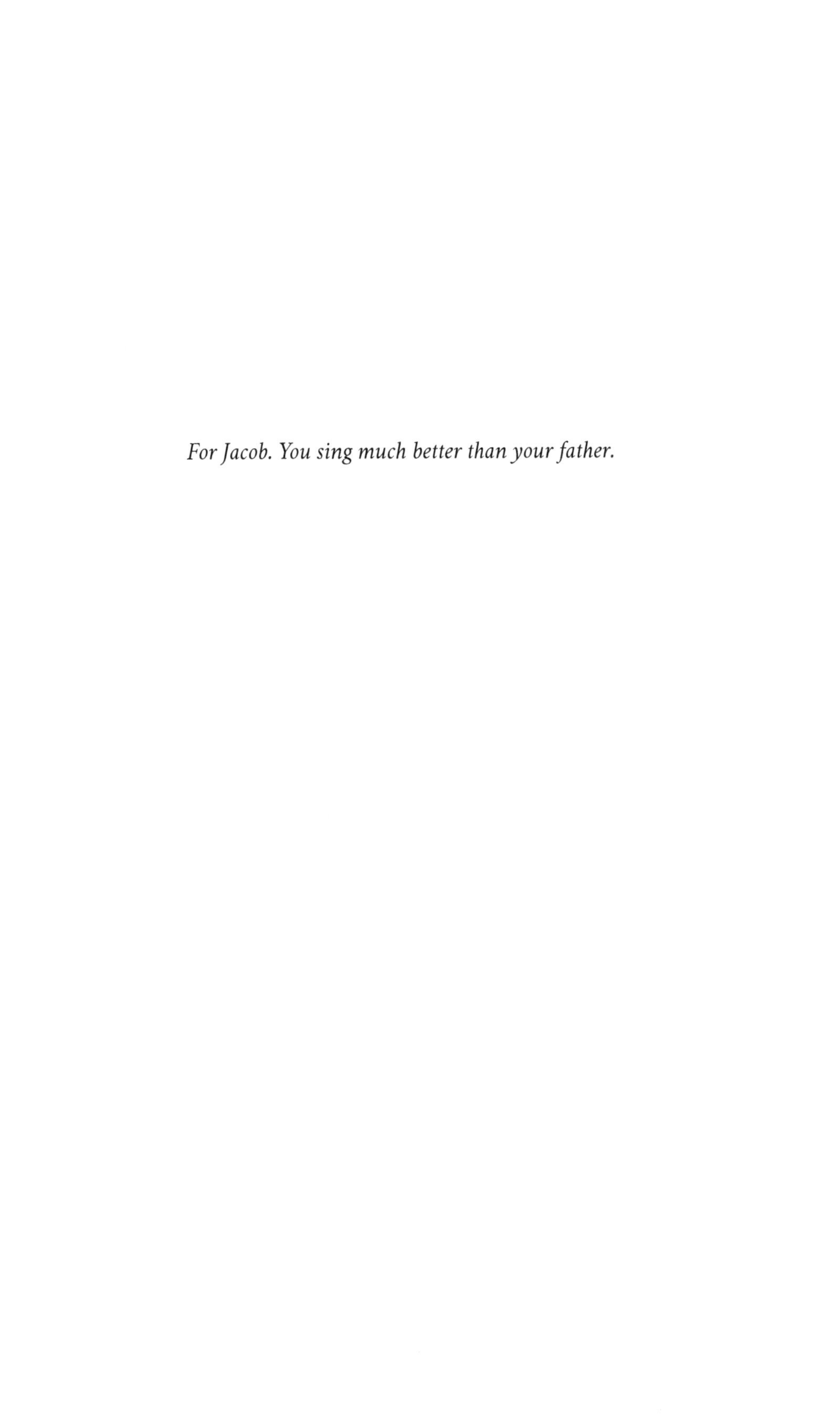

For Jacob. You sing much better than your father.

CONTENTS

MYTHS AND MAGIC

Bexley

A PAIR OF EYES STARES AT ME FROM BETWEEN TWO LARGE TREES IN THE middle of the dense forest behind our house. I stare right back, squinting through my binoculars to try to get a better look. I've never seen a female white-tail quite so large. I wish I could get a little closer so I could see her markings more clearly, but she's hidden well behind the leaves of the trees, and it's clear she's spotted me. If I make one wrong move, she's likely to bolt away, leaving me standing here staring at nothing but dense foliage. Still, I'm not seeing much at this angle, so perhaps I should hazard moving a little nearer.

Carefully, I inch forward, doing my best not to make a sound. I avoid the crunchy leaf piles that litter the ground. It's nearly winter; we should be having our first snow soon. Then, it will be easier to move undetected, but for now, I have to be careful.

I slide to my right, leaning up a bit onto my toes, and I can almost see her back clearly when I hear the crackle of a thousand leaves dying excruciating second deaths. Letting out a sigh, I turn to see my friend Fiona traipsing toward me, a wide grin on her face.

"There you are!" she squeals, rushing over with her arms wide open. "Your mother said I might find you out here."

"Here I am." While I am annoyed that the deer has now shot off into the woods, likely to never be seen again, I am happy to see Fiona. She's the first, and practically only, friend I've made since we moved to Luna Hollow almost a year ago. Her golden blonde hair catches the sun's light, creating a halo around her pretty face. She's beautiful in a traditional way, with bright blue eyes and perfectly shaped pink lips. Every young man in the kingdom is interested in making Fiona his wife someday. But since she's only nineteen, her parents aren't even entertaining the men who come knocking at her door.

I wish I was lucky in that regard as well.

With Fiona's arms around me, I squeeze her back. She finally releases me and straightens her blue cloak. I do the same to my dark green one. I try to blend into the trees the best I can when I come out here to observe the animals. It allows me to get closer to them—that and avoiding leaves.

"Why are you out here?" she asks, looking around. "It's so cold."

"I spotted a deer." I hear the excitement in my own voice. "You know how rare they've been lately. Before that, I saw a squirrel with a black patch of fur on its tail, and a flock of geese flew overhead."

Fiona practically rolls her eyes, but she's too polite to let me know how boring she thinks my animal investigations are. Instead, she just changes the subject. "You should be at home planning your birthday party, not standing out here freezing your toes off looking at wildlife."

"My birthday isn't until tomorrow," I remind her, slipping my binoculars back into my pocket. It would be rude of me to insist on continuing my investigations when she doesn't like it. We almost always do something Fiona likes to do, but that's okay. At least it gives me someone else to hang out with, other than my mother and my new stepfather, Harvey.

"I know your birthday isn't until tomorrow." Fiona loops her arm through mine, and we start walking back toward my house. Harvey's house sits on top of a hill surrounded by ten acres. It's a nice house— two stories with four bedrooms and indoor plumbing—and since most of the yard is covered in forest, I like it a lot more than I did our tiny apartment in our old home kingdom of Hexeton. I do miss my friends and my grandparents, but Hexeton is only about an hour-long carriage ride away, and we do visit sometimes, though not enough.

"So why must we discuss my birthday today?" I ask, brushing a long brown braid over my shoulder. I've never liked the color of my hair, but at least it matches my eyes.

"Because, as I've told you, you never know if you'll be allowed to stay at your home on your birthday or if you'll be summoned to the castle." A chill goes down Fiona's spine at her own words, and I can feel her shiver.

It has nothing to do with the bite in the wind either. She's genuinely afraid—afraid of being summoned to the castle for what's called King's Rite. I never heard of such a thing until I moved here. It all sounds so ridiculous to me. Why would some king who lives in a secluded castle at the top of a hill so high it's practically a mansion, surrounded by forests so thick I wouldn't even be able to see a deer five feet away, be interested in me? He probably doesn't even know I exist.

"Fiona," I begin, not for the first time, "I'm sure I will not be getting one of the infamous red letters in the mail you keep telling me about."

"You never know. My friend Samantha's sister got one just a month ago. She was gone all night, and when she came home, well, let's just say she wasn't the same."

I try not to scoff because I know this is a real concern for her, but to me, it sounds like something made up—like the legends about the witches in Hexeton. While plenty of old timers like to scare the kids by saying witches live in the woods around town, no one has ever seen one. No one I know has ever been affected by them.

So… until I see this king with my own eyes, I will not fear him. "I intend to celebrate my birthday tomorrow," I tell my friend. "Mother knows that."

"And what does your stepfather say?" We cross a little creek that crosses the yard about a hundred yards from the back of the house.

The bridge is only about four feet long, but I've always thought it was very pretty. In the springtime, I could stand here and watch the fish swim by underneath.

"He doesn't say much," I reply. The truth is, Harvey hardly speaks to me at all. Mother says that's just how he is—quiet. But I've seen him in a room full of people when he didn't stop talking plenty of times, so I don't think that's it. In my opinion, my stepfather simply doesn't care for me, and I suppose I can't blame him. After all, I was almost twenty years old when we met, a grown woman, and he'd gone his whole life without being a father. He leaves me alone for the most part, and I avoid him when possible. I do some work for his accounting firm, though, which he appreciates since I know he wishes I had a husband so I wouldn't be living off him any longer.

And he's doing everything he can to make that happen.

"Well, I think you should be on the lookout for that letter. If it's coming, it'll be in your mailbox in the morning. They just sort of appear overnight. No one has ever seen the person from the castle who brings them out," Fiona explains. "My friend Marcy knows someone who stayed up all night staring at her mailbox to see if they could catch a glimpse of the delivery person, but no one ever came. She was shocked when she opened her mailbox the next morning and the letter was inside."

A chuckle escapes my lips, and Fiona's eyes widen. "I was just thinking I shouldn't waste my time staring at the mailbox then if it won't matter."

"Bexley!" She shakes her head at me and marches up the steps toward my back door. "You have to take this seriously."

"I am," I tell her, but we both know that's not true. I follow her inside, and we hang up our coats. My mother absolutely adores Fiona, so she won't mind one bit if she spends time here.

"You are what?" Mother asks, wiping her hands on her apron as she comes over to greet both of us and give us a hug. "Your cheeks are so cold," she remarks as she pats my face.

"I'm nothing," I begin, taking a deep breath and savoring the delicious smell of my mother's famous vegetable stew.

But Fiona jumps in. "She's not taking the possibility of being summoned to the castle seriously," she tells my mother.

With a deep sigh, Mother goes to the cookie jar, opens it up, and extends it to Fiona. My friend squeals with delight and plucks out a chocolate chip cookie, taking a bite before she says thank you. I almost giggle at this, too. It's like we are still small children.

Cookie in hand, I sit at the table and wait for Mother to collect her thoughts. It's not like her to agree with such silly notions. She was always quick to dismiss any talk of witches in our town. She's a practical thinker, just like me.

So when she sits down across from me, Fiona to my left, and folds her hands, my forehead furrows. "I think we should celebrate your birthday tonight, Bex. Just in case."

My eyes lock on hers, so very similar to my own in color and shape, and I don't blink for a few moments. Finally, I manage to ask, "You do? Why?"

"Just in case." She shrugs one shoulder. "I've spoken to Harvey about it, and while he doesn't think there's any need to be alarmed about the situation, he says it does happen. Over the past seven years, quite a few young women who live in this village have gotten a letter from the king to appear in his castle on their birthday. It's happened in several villages throughout the kingdom, in fact, even in the older settlements on the other side of the mountain."

I'm not sure what to say, so I don't say anything at all. Instead, I finish my cookie.

Fiona jumps in on my behalf having already devoured her snack. She is one of those girls who can eat whatever she likes and always look perfectly fit. If I cared a smidge about my appearance, I might be jealous of her for that. "The girls who get the letter stay overnight," she says, her explanation similar to what she mentioned to me earlier as we were walking in. "When they come home, they can't speak about what happened to them there."

"That's what Harvey told me," Mother agrees. "But he also said that many of the girls have been examined by a physician afterward, and there's never anything physically wrong with them." She takes a deep breath and adds, "Those that went in maidens return as such."

I know I can speak to my mother about anything, but I don't like to talk about that sort of thing with her. I swallow hard and wait for Fiona to speak, as I know she will.

"But some of them have scratches and bruises. They say they can't remember how they got them." She turns and looks at me, her blue eyes piercing. "They simply have no idea where they've been or what's happened to them."

"Oh, please." I shake my head and wave one hand at her. "That has to be the king threatening them not to tell anyone."

"I don't think so," Mother chimes in. "Harvey seems to think that there are a few different ways it can be done but that a person's memory can be wiped."

"Magic?" I ask with a chuckle.

"No. He called it… hypnosis or something of that nature," she explains. "Don't ask me, dear. But you should plan on celebrating your birthday this evening. Now, would you like chocolate or vanilla cake?"

I look at Fiona, and she bats her eyelashes at me prettily, knowing she has won.

With a deep breath, I say, "Chocolate."

IT'S A YES FOR ME

Bexley

THE LAST REFRAINS OF HAPPY BIRTHDAY HANG IN THE AIR AS I SUCK IN a deep breath and blow out my candles. The small crowd that has gathered in the dining room to celebrate with us claps, and I force a smile to my face.

Our housekeeper, Mrs. Jones, takes the cake to cut it into slices while everyone claps. Glancing around at the faces before me, I see only a few genuine smiles. Mrs. Jones is giggling with glee, and I know she truly cares for me. She's become like a grandmother to me since I came here.

Of course, Mother and Fiona are happy, as well as Fiona's younger sisters Iris and Kate, who came over just for cake. But then I look at Harvey, and he's glowering. Harvey Moss has a stern face to match his bald head and his disposition, as well as his reputation as a no-nonsense accountant. I wouldn't cross him. I have no idea what Mother sees in him, but she only has kind things to say about her second husband.

And then I glance at Garth and wish I hadn't.

Garth Roberts sits at the other end of the dining room table, his muscular arms folded across his massive chest. He's easily six inches taller than Harvey and his shoulders are so wide he could probably easily wrap me around them. His dark hair is pulled back away from his face and tied with a ribbon, and his green eyes seem to bore through me as he watches me accept the slice of cake Mrs. Jones has set before me.

"Won't you have a piece, Garth?" Mother asks. She seemed a bit surprised when Harvey told her that he'd invited Garth for my birthday celebration, but she was always the perfect hostess. Even though Mother obviously wants what's best for me, I think she secretly wouldn't mind if I fell in love with Garth, married him, and started having some grandkids for her immediately. But she also knows I don't care for Mr. Roberts, so she doesn't try to force him upon me.

"Oh, no. I don't eat sweets," Garth says as I shuffle a large bite of chocolate cake into my mouth. He pats his flat stomach. "I wouldn't want to start to get fat. I wouldn't be able to keep up with the game if I did that."

My stomach roils as I am reminded of Garth's favorite pastime—hunting. I've heard he has the heads of several large animals hanging in his den, but I've never been in his house before. Not that he hasn't invited me. If Mother knew how strong he'd come on the last time he had me somewhat alone at a get-together, she'd toss him out on his ear.

I am probably meant to drop my fork at the implication that eating cake will make me fat. Instead, I scoop up an even bigger bite and shove it in my mouth, smearing chocolate across my teeth, and smiling at him.

He shakes his head, the sound coming from his throat one of disgust. I have to mark that as one small victory for me.

"Would you like a piece, dear?" Mother asks Fiona.

I know for a fact that Fiona loves Mother's chocolate cake. She's been talking about it all afternoon. So when she says, "Oh, no thank you. I'm still full from the stew," I wrinkle up my nose and prepare to tell her how horrid it is that she's let Garth's comments influence her.

I bite my tongue and glare at him instead.

Kate and Iris have no problem accepting the cake. Harvey takes a small piece, and Mother nibbles at one as well. I relish every bite of mine and then lick the fork before setting it down. If I really wanted to push Garth's buttons, I'd let out a belch, but I decide even the birthday girl can't get away with that sort of shenanigans.

"So, Becky," Garth begins, and I grimace. I've corrected him several times, but he insists that Bexley is a horrible name, so he must call me Becky instead. "What are your plans now that you're twenty-one?"

I open my mouth to answer, but Harvey speaks on my behalf. "She's been working at the firm a bit, part-time. She's actually quite good with numbers."

"Really?" Garth's eyebrows raise, and he slowly nods his head.

I'm not sure what's more offensive—that Harvey is shocked that I might be able to handle some basic math or that Garth is impressed by this.

"Yes. I am thinking of hiring her on full-time—to get her out of the house, of course. But... if she were to receive a marriage offer soon, well, that would be an even better situation for all of us."

I feel Mother's leg move under the table as she stiffens. I know she wants to speak up for me, but she won't. As much as she loves me, she respects her husband.

"I'm sure any eligible bachelor in town will be happy to have Becky as his wife," Garth begins, a crooked grin pulling up one side of his mouth. "She's very pretty, smart, and since she's relatively new to the village... mysterious."

"And I don't have any cavities." I narrow my eyes at him, offended as hell that he's now speaking about me as if I'm not even sitting here, as if I am chattel he can trade or barter for.

"Yes, well, as you know, it's the tradition for women to wait until after their twenty-first birthday, in honor of the king," Harvey explains.

"Oh, I know." Garth rolls his eyes and shakes his head. "I do find this entire affair utterly ridiculous."

Harvey's eyes shift to the side of his face, and his cheeks pink a bit. "It's not prudent to question the king, of course."

"Of course not." Garth scoffs, but I'm sure he doesn't mind if he offends the king. "Not that he ever leaves his castle to know what's happening here."

I do my best not to spend time with Garth when it can be avoided, but in the unfortunate times when I have been forced to listen to him speak, I've gotten the notion he's not too fond of King Canaan Zephyr. I'm not exactly sure why, but I heard him mention that the land where our village sits, and all of the area on this side of the mountain, was taken unfairly a few decades ago, that before then our territory was independent of either the kingdom of Luna Hollow to our east or Hexeton to our west. I don't know if that is true or not, but he seems to believe it is.

I've found that anything Garth believes is fact, and there's no use trying to persuade him otherwise.

"It's a good thing you didn't receive the red letter, Becky," Garth says to me. "A girl like you wouldn't be able to handle the trip to the castle."

I feel my stomach tighten into an even more severe knot. "Tomorrow is my birthday," I remind him. "We're celebrating early."

His mouth drops open. "Oh."

"You know they say you shouldn't take any chances," Harvey reminds him. "In case the girl gets the letter. You won't get to celebrate until she returns." He turns and looks at me. "If she returns." A cold, dead stare on his face, he pulls the corners of his mouth into a smile I can only describe as creepy.

I smile right back. "I seriously doubt the king even knows I exist," I admit. "I've only been here for a year or so, and I'm hardly consequential."

"That much is true," Garth says, leaning back in his chair so far the front two legs come off the floor. I'd love to see him topple over, but he won't. "Well, I'm not too worried about it. The king has never kept a girl for more than one night. Of course, the girls who are returned are blemished, and it's difficult for them to find a husband." He shakes his head. "The king has some nerve forcing himself on innocent girls."

"There's never been any evidence of the girls not being… intact when they return." Harvey's jumping in is certainly not meant to defend the girls in question so much as it is to assure my prospective suitor that I will still be a virgin when I come back from the castle, if I am taken.

Garth shrugs. "That's what they say, but honestly, how would anyone know?"

"Myra Pierce got married a few weeks after she came back," Fiona offers, her voice sounding overly sweet as she speaks to Garth. She's told me she thinks he's handsome. I guess pretty much everyone in the town does. The girls that grew up enamored with him can't see what a pig he is. "And then there's Susie Butler who—"

He waves a dismissive hand. "I really don't think it's going to be an issue." He looks at me coldly. "As Becky said, the king won't even know about her. She'll be fine."

"Well," Mother begins, pressing her hands to the table before she pushes up from her chair, "it has been so lovely having all of you over. You ladies should get home before it gets too late."

"I'll walk you," Garth offers. "It's the gentlemanly thing to do." He stands and looks at me again. "Sorry I didn't bring you a present, Becky, but I didn't know it was your birthday until your father came by a few hours ago."

"It's not a problem, Garth." I do my best to copy Fiona's pretty smile as I bat my eyelashes at him and stand. "The fact that you're leaving is present enough."

He must hear me wrong because his grin widens even as Harvey grunts in my general direction. "Everyone enjoys spending time with Garth."

"I'm sure that's true somewhere," I continue, walking along with everyone except for Harvey who trails far behind as we enter the living room and head toward the door. "It is a fairly common name."

This time, he seems to catch on that maybe I'm not flattering him.

His bushy eyebrows nearly touch as he stares at me for a long moment.

Everyone says their goodbyes. I hug Fiona and her sisters and thank them for coming. Fiona gave me a lovely painting of a rabbit earlier, which I intend to hang in my room, so I thank her again.

"Can I have a quick word with you on the porch, Becky?" Garth says, slipping his coat on.

"Aren't you walking the girls home?" I ask, confused.

He nods. "It'll only take a moment."

Mother hands me my coat, and I step outside with him. Fiona and her sisters wait in the yard as I stand by the door. At least Garth's girth prevents the full force of the autumn wind from chilling me as I wait to see what he has to say.

"I've spoken to your father, and he's agreed that we would be a good match."

I blink several times, my mouth suddenly dry. I manage to ask, "When did you speak to my father?"

"Earlier today." He grins at me.

"That would prove to be a bit difficult since he passed away when I was four." I fold my arms. What is the matter with this man? Is he really that stupid, or does he simply not care about tact?

Rather than looking embarrassed, he chuckles. "No, not that father. This one. Harvey."

"My stepfather," I remind him. I've known Harvey only a few weeks longer than I've known Garth, which isn't long. He shouldn't have much of a say over my life.

And yet, here we are.

"Anyway, I'll be by tomorrow afternoon with your ring."

My eyes widen, and he leans down to kiss my cheek. When he straightens, he's still grinning like the fool he is. He walks away, Fionna, Iris, and Kate following him like ducklings.

I stare after them wondering when the hell I said I'd marry him.

SUMMONED

Bexley

THE IDEA THAT SOMETHING IS IMPORTANT FLUTTERS BEHIND MY CLOSED eyelids as I lie in my bed, trying to pull my entire brain out of sleep. It's a losing battle. All I want to do is roll over and fall back into a peaceful slumber.

But that nagging feeling that I have something I need to do won't allow me to, and a few seconds later, I sit up in bed and push my blankets down to my waist.

It's my birthday.

Not only that, but it's my twenty-first birthday.

It's my twenty-first birthday, and I now live in some crazy kingdom where the king sometimes sends out letters to girls on their twenty-first birthday summoning them to the castle so he can… well, no one knows exactly what he does with them, but none of the villagers approve of it or thinks it's proper.

I take a deep breath and swing my feet out of bed. The wooden floor is a bit chilly, but I don't pause to put on my slippers. Instead, I shuffle into the bathroom, do my business, and throw on a clean dress. I run a brush over my teeth and another through my hair before poking my feet into my boots and heading downstairs.

Mother is up already. That's not too much of a surprise since she often gets up to prepare breakfast for Harvey, but the sun has barely met the top of the tree line, which means it's not even 6:00 in the morning. She stands near the front window wringing her hands, not in the kitchen where one would need to be in order to cook.

Her eyes are glued to the mailbox.

"How long have you been standing here?"

The sound of my voice startles her. She clutches her heart and turns toward me. "Oh, Bexley. You're awake. How did you sleep, dear?" As I approach, she reaches up to straighten my hair and pat my cheek.

"Fine." It's not a lie. While it did take me a while to fall asleep, once I did, I slept like a baby.

"Good, good. I've just been standing here for a few moments… looking at the sky. Do you think it will rain today?"

I look at the sky in question and see a hazy gray color that tells me it's a possibility, but then, the sun's not all the way up. No bright patches of pink and orange light the horizon today. Whether it rains or not, it's bound to be gloomy. Happy birthday to me.

"I don't know," I admit, going along with her story. I don't think there's any chance she's actually looking at the sky and not the mailbox. "You didn't see anyone deliver anything?"

She shakes her head. "No, but the post doesn't usually come until later in the day," she reminds me.

"True, but Fiona said that this letter, if it's coming, should be here first thing in the morning, and no one ever sees who delivers it." I shrug. Saying that story out loud seems so silly to me. It's not as if I believe it could be true. Just because some older people still believe in magic, that doesn't mean that I should.

Mother inhales deeply, her bottom lip shaking slightly. "Perhaps we should check then. Honestly, Bexley, I've been standing here for a while. I couldn't sleep."

My mouth turns down in a frown as I consider what she's saying.

"Oh, Mother." I place my hand gently on her shoulder. She's always been such a good parent to me. She loves me so much, and I absolutely don't know what I'd do without her. We've been close my entire life, but losing my father to an accident when I was so young made us grow even closer. For so many years, we only had one another.

Now, she has Harvey, and while I am jealous at times and often think he doesn't deserve her, I am glad she has someone else. While I highly doubt I'm about to be carted off to a castle on top of the mountain, I do hope one day to start a family of my own or at least a career. I'd love to work on a nature preserve or even a zoo, so it's important for Mother to put some space between us.

She wraps her arms around me. "I love you so much, Bexley. I don't know what I'd do without you."

I kiss her cheek. "You'll always have me,' I promise her. "We might not always live under the same roof, but I'm not going anywhere, Mother. I'll always be in your heart, and you'll be in mine."

When she looks at me again, she has tears in her eyes. She nods. "I know, baby. I know. Now, why don't you go see if there's anything in that mailbox?"

"Sure." I shrug, pretending like it's not a big deal. Taking my cloak from the hook by the door, I slip it into place and clasp it, taking my time. My hands shake slightly as I reach for the doorknob and step outside.

The scent of woodsmoke fills my lungs. I pause for a moment on the front porch, letting the sharp sting of the wind ground me. I'm here—at my house—my mother is inside watching. I'm fine. Everything is fine. There's no letter looming in the mailbox. No carriage will show up with some hooligan inside to snatch me up and carry me off to the castle, never to be seen or heard from again.

The autumn breeze stirs the leaves, lifting the few remaining red and orange ones off the ground and sending them twirling as I cross the front yard to the road where the mailbox stands sentinel. Why am I so frightened of a tiny black box I've seen the postal carrier fill hundreds of times? I have no idea. It is silly, really.

When I get to the mailbox, I position myself in front of it so that I can see the house in the distance. Mother lifts a hand to wave at me reassuringly as she looks through the front window. I wave back, but I don't feel the reassurance she is hoping to pass on to me.

I'm honestly downright terrified.

"It's empty," I whisper as I grab the door lever and pull it down hard.

Only... it's not empty.

My mouth drops open in a silent gasp as I stare at the red envelope tucked inside of the mailbox. It's large, weighty. Imposing. I can tell that before I even touch it.

I'm afraid to touch it.

In gold ink, my name is written, the script is fancy, with lots of curls, such that I can barely read it at an angle. With a heavy sigh, I reach in and slide it out.

"Bexley Kessler" it reads.

"Well, at least the king knows that Harvey isn't my father."

The door to the house flies open, and Mother comes running out onto the porch, nearly tripping. "Is it—"

"I believe so." My voice sounds so calm, I hardly recognize it. With the letter in my hand, I begin to walk toward her, thinking we can open it together. Each step feels like I'm walking through thick quicksand that threatens to suck me down into the center of the earth.

I'm not sure it would be a worse option.

A thousand thoughts of what may happen to me fill my mind. I've never even kissed a man before. What if the tales about those other women aren't true, and the king really does take his turn with the girls who have just stepped freshly into adulthood?

Eventually, I manage to make it to the porch. Mother takes the letter from my hand and carries it inside. Mrs. Jones is awake now. She's wearing a thick blue robe over her nightgown as she stands near the fireplace with her hands clasped.

I note that Harvey hasn't bothered to wake up early on my account.

Mother sinks down on the sofa but offers me the letter. "You should do it."

I want to joke that maybe if she opens it, she'll be the one that has to go, but no one would think that funny at the moment. I sit on the edge of the cushion next to her and slide my finger under the cell. The letter is beautiful, and it seems a shame to tear it up. The flap gives, revealing a sheet of thick white paper with embossed print.

I think it's probably a form letter all the girls get until I see that it's actually handwritten and contains my name.

"Miss Bexley Kessler, you are hereby summoned to meet with your king, His Royal Highness Canaan Zephyr, this evening at seven o'clock. A carriage shall arrive to retrieve you at six o'clock. As your stay will be at least one night, possibly more, pack accordingly." The bottom of the letter is signed Lawrence Wood, Esq.

"Who is Lawrence Wood?" I ask my mother.

She shakes her head, her eyes still brimming with tears as if I've received a death sentence. "I have no idea, but he seems important."

I suppose the esquire part tells us that.

"He is the king's top legal advisor," Harvey says, marching down the stairs in a neatly tied robe, the bottom of his pajamas peeking out above his slippers. "Mrs. Jones, coffee, please."

The housekeeper, who isn't usually the one to manage the kitchen, scurries off, and I can tell she's upset by the news of my inevitable departure as well.

Harvey is still fidgeting with his belt as he comes over and plucks the letter from my hands. He reads it, shakes his head, and holds it in his hand despite me reaching for it.

I'd like to have it back. Even though I don't like what it says, it still belongs to me.

"This ruins everything," he mutters, dropping the letter unceremoniously on the coffee table. "Now, Garth will have no use for you." He turns to look at me like I'm an alley cat eating out of a garbage can behind his office building.

Mother, though tentative, leaps into protective mode. "We don't know that," she says. "Garth seems awfully smitten with Bexley."

I stop the laugh that threatens to explode from my throat. He doesn't even call me by my real first name.

Mrs. Jones returns with a service of coffee with three mugs, but I'll not be having any. I have a lot to do today if I'm going to be ready to go at 7:00.

"What if she simply doesn't go?" Harvey asks. "What if we send her back to Hexeton for a week or so to stay with her grandparents? When they show up to collect her, we say she's not here?"

"Won't that just upset the king?" Mother asks, sitting down on the couch. Harvey claims a chair and begins to sip his coffee, making a face like it's not right. I decide I should sit as well, though I really just want to go outside and look for that deer again.

Harvey shrugs. "I doubt the king actually knows which women to expect. He's probably just waiting in his bedroom for someone. Surely, more than one girl in the kingdom turns twenty-one today."

"I have to go." My voice is just a whisper, but they both turn and look at me. Mother whimpers slightly. "I don't know how I know I have to go, but I know I do."

"You want to go?" Harvey looks at me as if I'm the most filthy creature in the world.

I shake my head. "No, but I have a feeling the king will find a way to make sure I'm there. Fiona says no one has ever gotten out of it once they've been summoned."

"Psh! Fiona! That girl is as daft as you are," Harvey says. "This will ruin everything." He sets his coffee down and flees the room, still muttering under his breath about how awful I am, the letter is, the world is.

Mother reaches over and takes my hand. "He didn't mean that."

"I know." Now, both of us are lying to one another. "I'm going to go outside for a bit."

She nods with tears threatening to fall again.

I don't worry about the crunch of the leaves as I approach the forest. It's only when I cross the line that separates the tangle of trees and undergrowth from the rest of civilization that I am careful. I've spent so much time here, I know all the trails, where the animals tend to hide, what they like to eat, everything. I've learned a lot about animals from my time in the forest, and I truly enjoy studying their habits. I wonder if I'll ever have a chance to put that knowledge to good use or if I will be banished after my return from the castle.

I'm just beginning to let my mind wander to what it might be like to meet the king when I see a pair of eyes staring at me from between the hedges. Golden and glowing, they're unlike anything I've ever seen before, and it takes my breath away.

This is definitely not the white-tail.

Most of the animals I've encountered have a level of intelligence behind their eyes, but this one is different. It's looking at me the same way a human would, as if it's trying to figure me out. Like it knows just as much as I do.

Part of me says this is a predator, and I should turn and run, but the rest of me is curious. What is this? It's too tall to be a fox or a wolf. I take a few steps closer, but then a cracking sound behind me has me turning around. I hear another animal take off through the brush, and when I turn back around, the eyes are gone.

"Who are you?" I whisper, but my only answer is a distant howl.

SWEPT AWAY

Bexley

At 5:45, I carry my suitcase down the stairs. Mother, Fiona, and Mrs. Jones stand there, tears in their eyes. I feel like a soldier being sent off to war. It's silly, really. I'll be fine.

I'll be back tomorrow.

I remind my mother of that. "Don't eat all the stew," I say with a smile. "I'll be wanting it for dinner tomorrow night."

She can barely speak as she leans over and kisses my cheek. "I'll… save some for you. I love you so much."

Now, she's making me tear up. "I love you, too, Mother." I kiss her back. "It'll be fine."

"No one ever stays more than one night," Fiona reminds us. "Really, it might be kind of nice to get to see the fancy castle. They used to have grand balls there. My grandmother went to one many years ago. You'll get to see all of that."

She's trying to be optimistic, and I appreciate it, but I can barely manage a smile.

A sharp knock on the door has us all jumping. Mrs. Jones takes a deep breath and opens it to reveal—just Garth.

"I heard about the letter," he says solemnly, shaking his head. Turning to me, he adds, "I wanted to come see you off, Becky."

"Thank you." He's the last person I want to see at the moment, but the sound of his voice coaxes Harvey from his study so that now there are two people I don't want to see here. They shake hands and begin to chat about hunting, a sport I detest that Garth's entire life apparently revolves around.

No matter what happens to me at the castle, I am not a good match for Garth. Perhaps the king will be doing me a favor by ruining my reputation.

A clip-clopping sound has my stomach lurching into my throat. I peer out the window as Mother's shaky hands position my cloak around my shoulders.

I see a carriage coming up the drive. It's large and ornate. All of the neighbors come out of their houses and stand along the cobblestone road, trying to get a look. "They should've brought binoculars," I mutter, feeling like a spectacle.

The carriage stops in front of our house, and a very regal looking man steps out. He's wearing a suit with his dark hair slicked back. Massive shoulders and muscular arms tell me this man is no one to argue with. If he says get in the carriage, one gets in the carriage.

"Is that him?" I whisper to Fiona. "Is that the king?"

"I don't think so. No one ever sees the king anymore," she mutters. "Not since he was the prince."

I don't know what that means, and I don't have time to ask. A footman accompanies the gentleman to the door and knocks for him. My palms are sweaty as I turn the knob and pull it open.

A smile lights his handsome face, his green eyes gleaming. "Miss Bexley Kessler?"

All I can do is nod my head.

He bows a bit as he says, "I'm Ellison Lake, here to accompany you to the castle." He seems polite and kind, and with such empathy in his eyes, I'm inclined to step forward and let him lead me away.

My plans are ruined when Garth steps forward, nearly knocking me into the wall. "And just who may you be?" His voice is authoritative, as if Mr. Lake is somehow infringing upon something that belongs to him.

Mr. Lake is a bit taller than Garth and broader, which is saying something because I've never imagined a man could be bigger than Garth. He clears his throat, but his charming disposition doesn't waiver. "I'm an advisor to the king," he says with a smile. "And you are?" He lifts a hand, and I imagine him crushing a watermelon in his palm.

Garth tentatively shakes Mr. Lake's hand. "I'm Garth Roberts, Becky's betrothed."

My eyes bulge, and my stomach twists into a knot. I hear my mother gasp behind me, and Harvey chuckles low in his throat as if he thinks Garth's claim will prevent the king from taking me away.

Mr. Lake's forehead crinkles as he looks at me. "We have no record of any upcoming nuptials at the castle."

All I can do is shake my head slightly, and I get the feeling that, somehow, Mr. Lake understands what I am thinking.

"Well, that's simply because we only became engaged last night," Garth replies, folding his arms across his chest, his chin in the air.

With a nod, Mr. Lake takes my suitcase from my hand. "I see. Well, I'm afraid anything that hasn't been filed with the proper authorities won't prevent Miss Kessler's visit to the castle."

"But… the king cannot possibly expect for me to make her my bride after he… defiles her!" Garth spits.

Horror washes over me as I wait for Mr. Lake to throw the first punch in defense of the king. Garth has no problem whatsoever speaking ill of the king. That's one thing behind closed doors, possibly even in the middle of town amongst the right people, but this man is obviously very close to the king.

Clearing his throat, Mr. Lake says, "I'm sure you've heard rumors about what happens in the castle, but I can assure all of you that no defiling is about to happen." When his eyes reach mine, they are full of warmth and understanding. Despite the uncertainty of my plight, I do believe him.

Garth does not. A rumble explodes from his chest. "You expect us to believe that?"

"I honestly couldn't care less what you believe." Mr. Lake is beginning to lose his patience. One of the horses snorts and stomps its foot. That's not a coincidence. Animals can sense human emotion, and this one knows there's an issue. "Now, Miss Kessler, if you've said your goodbyes, let us be on our way." Mr. Lake offers his arm and I take it.

Garth follows us onto the porch. "This isn't right, you know! Does he understand what everyone is saying about him? That he's a perverted, egotistical—"

"Garth!" Harvey steps in as I feel Mr. Lake's arm tense under my hand. "Please. You mustn't speak ill of the king."

Rather than turn around and pound him in the face, Mr. Lake simply keeps walking.

I turn my head to peer past where Harvey is trying to calm Garth before everyone gets arrested and see my mother and Fiona weeping and waving. I lift a hand and manage a smile, but the fear I've felt bubbling inside of me all day rises to the surface, and I'm afraid I might burst into tears myself.

"In we go," Mr. Lake says, handing my suitcase to one of the footmen as he directs me inside of the carriage. I sit on one side, and he manages to fold himself through the narrow door and take a seat across from me.

I run my hands over the plush velvet seat. It's a rich blue that practically screams royalty. Ornate gold scrollwork climbs the walls. It's beautiful and comfortable in here. Even with the large stranger sitting across from me, I feel safe.

A moment later, the carriage begins to move. I'm inclined to open the curtain and look back at Mother and the others, but I don't. I think it's best if we just leave our goodbyes as they were spoken.

"I apologize," Mr. Lake says, drawing my attention to his warm eyes again. "This is never easy." I can tell by the way his shoulders slump that he doesn't enjoy being the one to come and collect the women. I'm honestly surprised no one has ever mentioned him to Fiona. He seems quite memorable. "I try to avoid it when I can."

I nod, thinking maybe he isn't the usual aristocrat who goes out to collect the women then. "I'm sorry—about Garth," I stutter, wanting to pour everything out to him but thinking it unnecessary. Still, he should know, "My parents fully support the crown."

A crooked smile pulls at one side of his mouth. "A lot of people question the crown these days. You will get the opportunity to see why. However, I'm afraid it won't last long. When you leave, whenever that is, you won't remember what you've experienced at the castle."

A chill runs the length of my spine. "How is that possible?"

His smile broadens. "We have our ways."

"Does it hurt?"

He chuckles, a soothing baritone that calms me instantly. "No. Nothing painful or uncomfortable will happen to you. Well, not physically anyway." He runs a hand through his mop of unruly dark hair.

I'm not sure what that means, but I decide not to ask. I wish I could see out the window. I can only imagine what kind of wildlife we might see out the window as we approach the forest. It is dark out, but the moon hangs high in the sky this time of year, and I'm certain I might see an owl.

Or a wolf.

"What do you like to do in your free time, Miss Kessler?"

He's trying to set me at ease, and I appreciate it. "I like animals," I tell him, and he nods as if he somehow already knew that. "I like to observe them. To study them."

"Interesting, and do you think you might make a career out of that one day?" Unlike Garth, he seems genuinely interested.

I shrug. "I'd like to, but my stepfather has me working in his firm more and more recently. I don't mind working with numbers. I'm quite good at math. But I would prefer to be outside."

"And your betrothed?" He says the word like we both understand that's not what Garth is. "What does he do?"

I shake my head. "Other than call me by the wrong name?"

Mr. Lake chuckles again, and I can imagine many a woman doing all she can to cause him to make that sound.

Thinking of Garth does not make me want to laugh, though. "He is a local hunter and also owns a farm and some other businesses. I honestly don't know that much about him. I've only met him a few times."

He nods in understanding. "He seems close with Mr. Moss."

"Mr. Moss would like for him to be." I take a deep breath, inhaling his spicy cologne. I briefly wonder about the king. If his advisor looks and acts like this, how much more handsome and charming must he be? "I haven't lived here long; well, about a year, but most of the villagers have grown up together, attending the same schools and such. I have struggled to make friends. Other than Fiona." He continues to nod as I talk about how we moved to Luna Hollow because my mother met Harvey through a mutual friend, and I never really wanted to come, but I love my mother and want her to be happy. I've probably been talking for ten minutes when I say, "I'm so sorry, Mr. Lake. I shouldn't be rambling on."

"Please, call me Ellison," he says in that casual tone. "And you're not rambling. All of that is quite interesting to me. Tell me more about Hexeton."

I'm not sure if he's just trying to distract me or if he really wants to know, but I tell him about the kingdom I grew up in. "The king died before I was born, and since he had no children, it's just the queen now."

He nods, and I should realize he already knows that. "Queen Maeve."

"That's right. She made a lot of public appearances when I was younger, but as she aged, she stopped coming out so much. I'm not sure what will happen when she passes away." He only shrugs. I decide it's time to stop talking about politics, so I move on to tell him about my grandparents' house and how much I loved spending time there.

"These are your father's parents?" he asks me.

"Both," I say. "I mean... I loved going to both sets of grandparents' houses. But yes, my father's parents have a large forest behind their property. So of course I loved that. Grandpa would go out with me sometimes to look for animals. And Grandma would bake us something warm and delicious to eat when we got home."

His smile is genuine. "Do you remember much about your father?"

I hesitate, not sure what I can share with this man, but then I nod, and his smile widens.

PRINCESS OR PRISONER?

Bexley

"My father died in an accident when I was quite young," I begin. "Mother says it happened very quickly. He was only twenty-three."

"I'm sorry for your loss. Do you know what happened?"

Again, I shake my head. "No. Mother doesn't like to talk about it. I only know it happened deep in the woods."

"Interesting." He strokes his chin leaving me to ponder what's so interesting about that. "We are beginning to climb the hill to the castle now. Would you like for me to open the curtain so you can see the forest?"

"Yes! I'd love that." My enthusiasm would be embarrassing if I didn't feel so comfortable with him.

Ellison laughs and pulls the curtain back on both sides of the carriage. I oscillate between each of them, doing my best to peer through the darkness into the trees. The road is narrow enough that tree branches occasionally scrape the top. We roll over some deep ruts that jar me out of my seat, and one of them makes me bump my nose on the window.

"Are you all right?" he asks. "I'm so sorry."

"I'm fine." I rub it and continue to look out. I see a large bird in the top of the tree and several small creatures skitter by. Mother always marvels at how good I am at finding animals, but sometimes I think they find me.

"The road needs repair," Ellison mutters. I spare a glance at him, but then my focus is out the window again. "We could fix it, but then, people might be inspired to use it."

Again, I glance over my shoulder and see him dragging a hand down his face. He meets my eyes and realizes he's said too much.

"I won't remember any of this tomorrow," I remind him, and he looks relieved. I turn my head back to the window, but then I have to ask myself what the point is. Nothing I see will stick with me.

"It makes you happy now," he says, as if he's reading my mind.

He's not wrong, so I go back to looking for animals. We have just leveled off when we pass through a large gate. Cast iron and marble, it's impressive, but what's even more breathtaking is the sight of several pairs of eyes gleaming through the dark forest on the other side of the gate. "Are those wolves?"

He scoots toward me and looks out at the eyes. "Possibly." He seems nonchalant. "A lot of animals live in the woods around the castle—on both sides of the fence. I don't recommend going out there."

Again, I look into his eyes and see that this is a warning. I nod. I can't imagine why I ever would.

Even after we pass through the gate, it takes a few minutes for the carriage to begin to slow down. We are in a clearing now, and the magnificent yard comes into view first. Despite the darkness, I can see the perfectly manicured grass. It appears to be a deep green with every blade in place. Then, the hedges come into view, and they are also immaculate.

"You should see the garden in the back of the castle. There's a labyrinth, several fountains, and all kinds of beautiful flowers, especially roses. The queen loves—loved—roses." He clears his throat, and

I can't tell if it's sorrow at having mentioned the late queen that makes him do so or something else.

"I'd love to see that," I tell him as we pull up in front of a huge building made of the same white marble that the gate supports were made from.

I can't see much of it from here. We're at such an odd angle, but as the footman opens the door, I step out and look up. It's massive—tall and imposing—with turrets and ledges. All of it seems to be sculpted out of one continuous piece of white marble.

Ellison steps out next to me. "It's intimidating, but don't worry. Almost everyone inside is quite lovely and kind."

I arch an eyebrow. "Almost everyone?"

He shrugs one shoulder and offers his arm. I take it. "Those who are not won't have much to do with you anyway, I'm sure."

I grip his arm tighter. We walk inside, and the interior is even more breathtaking than the outside. Everywhere I look, expensive pieces of art fill the walls. The floor is polished white marble that gleams beneath crystal chandeliers. I'm fully aware that my continuous gasp is probably quite annoying, yet I can't help myself. We glide across the floor about halfway toward a grand stairwell when an older gentleman wearing a butler's uniform and a woman who instantly reminds me of Mrs. Jones appear in front of us.

"Miss Kessler—" Ellison begins.

"Oh, it's Bexley," I say, realizing I never told him to call me by my first name the way that he had asked me to.

"Bexley." He grins, and I feel myself melt just a little on the inside. He's so charming! "This is Anna. She'll be taking care of you during your stay. She's our head housekeeper and the kindest soul you'll ever meet."

Anna gives me a grandmotherly smile and a nod, and I believe every word he's said.

"And this is David, our head butler. While he's not quite as sweet as Anna, if you need anything at all, you can ring for him, and he'll be there to help you. Anna will show you to your room so you can freshen up, and then I'll take you in to introduce you to the king before supper."

My eyes widen slightly at the notion of meeting the king, but I nod. He pats my arm, and then he's gone.

"Hello, dear." Anna's voice is as sweet as her smile. "This way, dear."

I look around for my bag. David says, "The footman has delivered your luggage to your room." His smile is also inviting. I nod a thank you and then follow along as Anna leads me up the stairs.

We seem to climb forever, but it doesn't even make her catch her breath. By the time we get to whatever floor my room is on, I feel like my lungs are on fire. "This way." She turns a corner, and I only have a moment to appreciate the art on the walls and the view out the window before she comes to a stop in front of a pair of ornate doors.

When she opens them, it reveals the most beautiful bedroom I've ever seen. I gasp and hesitate on the threshold, not sure if I should follow her inside or not.

The large four poster bed is full of carvings from the headboard to the footboard. It's painted white to help lighten the room, as is the rest of the furniture. I see the faces of forest animals in the wood, as well as the artwork that hangs over the large fireplace where a fire blazes, and across the other walls. The light blue wallpaper has a feminine pattern in cream. In the center of the ceiling hangs another crystal chandelier, but this one is far more feminine than others I've seen throughout the castle.

This looks like a bedroom fit for a princess, so I can't see myself staying here, not even for one night.

"Well come in, darling," Anna coaxes. "This is where you'll be staying. You'll find a wardrobe full of gowns over there." She gestures across the room. "I'm sure you'll find something to your liking for supper."

I stare at her for a moment wondering how they know my measurements. Do they just keep a variety of sizes on hand for all the women who stay here?

When I think of the other girls who have likely stayed in this same room, some of the specialness I'd been feeling melts away. It's silly. Of course, they didn't prepare all of this for me. Why would they? Even if the animal touches do seem fitting. Maybe the entire castle is just decorated that way and it's a coincidence.

"Here are the call boxes," she says, walking over to the wall near the bed. "You just press this button and speak into the tube, and one of the staff members will hear you and send me up. This one is for David." She moves her hand slightly to the left. "Of course, in the unlikely event no one responds, there's always the bell." She doesn't pull the chord but shows me the bell, and I nod.

"Thank you for all of your kindness."

"Of course!" She comes to me and pats my arm. "Your suitcase is just over there." She points to the armoire, and I see it nestled in the corner. "Let me know if you need anything. Supper is at nine."

That seems awfully late to me, but I only nod. Thankfully, I had a bit of Mother's stew before we left.

Once Anna departs, I take a moment to enjoy the room. The bed is super comfortable. All the pillows are squishy, and the mattress is heavenly. The blankets are soft and inviting.

I don't stay lying down too long, though. I rush to the window and look out at the forest. I can see the trees in the distance, but it's too far to make out much. I bet if I stand there long enough, eyes will appear.

There's no time for that right now, though. I throw open the armoire and peer inside. A thousand dresses in every shade imaginable greet me, making me gasp in shock and wonder. I pull out one skirt after another to look at them and finally settle on a light blue gown the color of the bedroom walls. I figure the king must like blue since his carriage is this color as well as this room, not that he's ever spent much time in here.

A shudder goes down my spine. Or has he?

I look at the bed and try to remember what Ellison said to Garth. There will be no deflowering today. Still, can Ellison know everything?

It will do me no good to worry about it, so I get dressed like I am a princess for the night. It is still my birthday, after all. I manage to get into the gown by myself and sit at the dressing table to fix my hair. All the fancy products lined up there are remarkable, and I want to sample every one of them. By the time it's five minutes until 9:00, I look like a different person. I've used a bit of blush, dark eye shadow, and coral colored lipstick. I smell like strawberries. Standing, I take one last look in the mirror and decide I'm ready to meet the king. I hope Ellison will be there with me because I'm already beginning to think of him as a friend.

His sharp knock on the door is distinguishable, so I'm not surprised when I throw it open and find him standing there looking regal in an even fancier suit. His tie is the same shade of blue as my dress.

"Twinsies!" he says, and I burst out laughing.

"How did you know?"

He shrugs. "I took a guess. Are you ready?" He offers me his arm, and I take it.

"Yes, but I am a little nervous."

"Don't be," he says with a dismissive wave. "Everyone gets so worked up to meet the king, and then it's really nothing."

I wonder if that's because I won't remember it. Still, I'm not good at making small talk. "I have no idea what to say to him."

"Honestly, something along the lines of, 'It's a pleasure to meet you, Your Highness,' with a curtsy is probably enough."

"For an entire dinner?" I ask, almost stopping in my tracks to look at him.

"Oh, he won't be eating dinner with us. That'll just be the two of us and a few of his advisors. The king never takes his meals with anyone," Ellison explains.

Now, I do pause to turn in his direction. "He doesn't?"

"No. We will stop by his office on the way to the dining room. I'll introduce you, and then I'll escort you to dinner. That'll be the extent of your interaction, at least for tonight."

My forehead crinkles, but when he starts walking again, I go along. "Is there some sort of time continuum here?" I ask, almost laughing at the absurdity of the question. I don't believe in magic, but I do believe in science. Is that possible?

"No, why?" He chuckles, and I momentarily feel better.

"Because everyone says it'll just be one night, but then you made it sound like I might see him again tomorrow," I reply.

"Well, he's never kept any of the birthday girls for more than one night," Ellison says. "But we can't rule it out."

I feel my heart sink to my feet. As beautiful as it is here, and as kind as everyone has been, the idea that I might not be reunited with my mother tomorrow has me feeling forlorn.

"Don't worry. I'm sure it'll be fine," Ellison tells me. We head down the stairs in silence and down a maze of hallways until we reach what feels like the back of the castle to me. Here, the white marble seems to dim to something more akin to gray slabs of stone. The lights are dimmer, and the artwork turns more bleak. Images of dark forests and scary looking castles hang on the walls. Busts of dragons and other monsters sit on pillars, and the shadows thicken around us.

We reach an imposing door, and Ellison wraps, still forcing a smile.

It takes a moment before we hear a rumbling, "Enter."

My breath catches in my throat, and I squeeze Ellison's arm so tight I might injure a lesser man. We step inside a dark room where only a few candle sconces along the walls give us any sort of illumination. Thick dark curtains cover the windows, and in the far reaches, back in the darkest shadows, I make out the outline of a large desk and a chair, which is facing away from us.

A chill runs up my spine, and it has nothing to do with the garish fireplace adorned with gargoyles being unlit. The man in that chair frightens me, and it's all I can do to get my feet moving.

"Your Majesty," Ellison says, his voice unwavering, "may I present Miss Bexley Kessler of Menschen Village."

I clear my throat, and as the chair swivels slowly around, I squeak out, "It's an honor to meet you, Your Maj—"

I can't finish the word. Yellow gold eyes stare back at me from the darkness. A scream lodges in my throat, and I feel compelled to tear myself away from Ellison, to run away, and never come back.

SHE'S THE ONE

CANAAN

THE GIRL STANDS WITH HER NAILS EMBEDDED INTO ELLISON'S ARM SO deeply, if he wasn't wearing a suit jacket, he'd probably be bleeding. Her eyes are wide in horror as she takes me in, and I can't blame her. Any moment now, she'll scream and rush from the room.

Somehow, she manages to eke out the rest of her statement, "Your Maj—esty," and keep her feet planted firmly in place. I am impressed. She's lasted longer in the same room with me than everyone else.

But then, I realized there was something different about this girl as soon as I saw her name on my list. I'd gone to see for myself earlier this morning, something I've never done before. I'd felt how special she is the moment our eyes locked—not here in my office, but in the woods outside her home.

"Bexley," I growl, the sound of my own voice making my skin crawl. "Pleasure. You may go."

Ellison stands there a moment longer. He's never had to actually escort a girl from my office before because they have always taken off running before he had the chance. Through the mind-link I say, *"Go, El."*

"Yes, of course, Alpha." He blinks a few times and then leads her out of the room. I wait until the door closes to let out a somber breath. With her gone, I turn on the lamp on my desk. My vision in the dark is better than any other creature on the planet, but I still need the light to see fine detail. I look at her photograph and go over the details from her file again.

"Bexley," I mumble. "What kind of a name is that?" No one is around to answer my question, and that's just fine. I prefer to keep it that way.

She's strikingly beautiful, with chestnut hair that falls around her shoulders in waves. Her doe-eyes are brown and warm, and the angles of her face are sharp, just like her intellect. A hollowness fills the center of my chest just looking at her and imagining what might've been if I hadn't been handed my fate all those years ago.

Letting out a sigh, I close the folder and set it aside. It doesn't matter. Nothing I say or do will ever lift this curse. I should be happy at having found Bexley. The rest of the castle will be so full of hope if I tell them the truth. They'll want to do everything they can to convince her to stay. I turn to look at the calendar hanging on the wall and note I only have eighty-seven more days until my twenty-fifth birthday; I'm running out of time.

But not even a thousand days would be enough to convince Bexley to see past what I've become. I lift a mangled paw and run it through the fur on the top of my head. Not a wolf, not a human, I am trapped in-between. I can't even bear to look at my own reflection. How can I expect anyone else to want to look at me?

She'll be down the hallway back in the light area of the castle with Ellison and the others now, enjoying her supper and trying to forget about the hideous creature she just encountered. The problem is, unlike the others, Bexley will never forget me, which could be quite problematic when she returns home. I'll have to find some other way to make sure she doesn't tell the people in her village what she's seen. After all, no one could possibly swear fealty to a monster like me. The whispers in the villages, particularly the ones claimed by my father when I was younger, reach my ear, even though I haven't left the castle in over seven years. I know that these are troubling times. It would only take a few descriptive words from Bexley to inspire citizens to revolt against me.

Standing, I make my way over to the window and pull the curtains open slightly. In the distance, I can see the lights of the villages on the west side of the mountain. Those territories had previously been a buffer between our lands and the kingdom of Hexeton. But my father had foolishly claimed them as his own, despite the advice of his most trusted, wisest cabinet members telling him not to. The result is the mess we are in now.

I take a deep breath and lean my head against the cool glass. Winter is coming—in more ways than one. I have to be careful when I look through the window or else I'll catch my own reflection, and I don't need any more reminders of how hideous I am. Any notion I may have of attempting to keep Bexley here and convince her to fulfill her role in this mess goes out the window as I recall my gruesome fangs and creepy yellow eyes.

I could never ask anyone to do that—to try to love me.

Not even her—my mate.

Bexley

I sit at a table next to Ellison in the grandest dining room I've ever seen. The food is delicious, and everyone I've met is so kind and interesting, but I can't pay attention to any of it.

All I can think about is him—the king.

Terror swept over me as I took in the outline of his form. Cast against a backdrop of shadows, with only the faint illumination from the wall sconces in the distance, it had been difficult to see him at all.

Except for those glowing yellow eyes.

But in my mind, I can see his outline. I know that he is not human. At least, he's unlike any human I've ever seen before. I had no idea someone like him could ever even exist, and yet I've seen him with my own eyes.

He's seen me, too. Not just in the castle, but as I think about my encounter earlier today with the creature in the woods behind my house, I know for a fact that was him.

Why the king would come to my home to spy on me, I have no idea, especially when he knew I was coming here this evening. Yet, his eyes were exactly the same as the pair I'd seen in the forest earlier today. The height would be about the same, too, I imagine, if he were crouching in the woods, rather than sitting as he was in his office. It had to be him.

"Bexley?"

Ellison's voice lures me back to the table. I look up at him, a sheepish expression telling him that I have no idea what he's asked me.

He repeats himself. "Are you enjoying the lamb?"

"Oh, yes. It's delicious." I smile and take another bite. I notice that everyone sitting here has a lot of meat on their plates, even the dainty women. We don't eat a lot of meat in Menschen. It isn't that we don't enjoy it. Meat is hard to come by and expensive. Harvey is one of the wealthiest men in town and still doesn't spend a lot on meat. We eat a lot of stews and soups which incorporate local beef and goat, but it's been ages since I've had lamb. It is tasty, but I'm not inhaling it like the others.

"You work as an accountant?" a woman named Naomi asks. She is seated next to her husband, who was introduced to me as Dr. Justin Sands. She's probably a few years older than me with bright blonde hair and green eyes. In some ways, she reminds me of Fiona, and I imagine we could be friends if I were to stay here.

But I won't be staying here, thank goodness. It's clear the king wanted nothing to do with me. A ripple of disappointment passes through me with no origin whatsoever.

"That's right," I tell her, taking a sip of the best red wine I've ever tasted.

"Do you find it boring?" Olive, a brunette who sits on Justin's other side asks. "I think I'd go crazy having to fuss over all those numbers all day." She giggles, and I wonder if there's much going on in her head.

"Olive here has never been one for math," Ellison explains, shaking his head.

Olive narrows her eyes at him, and I wonder for a moment if perhaps they're a couple, but then she shakes her head, and I decide they're not.

"I don't mind math," I say. "Though I do prefer being outside when possible."

"What do you do when you're outside?" Justin takes another bite of lamb and chews it slowly, savoring it. My, these folks do enjoy their meat.

"Mostly, I go out into the forest to study the animals," I tell them, hearing the excitement in my own voice. "I just love them. Sometimes, I get lucky enough to pet a rabbit or have a bird land on my shoulder."

"Oh, how wonderful!" Naomi clasps her hands. "That would be nice. Every wild creature seems to be afraid of me." She looks at her husband and whispers, "Well, all but you."

Justin's eyes widen slightly, and he jabs her lightly in the ribs. I can't tell if it's an admonishment or not, but he doesn't seem thrilled that she's talking like that at dinner. She only giggles.

Ellison chuckles in the back of his throat again, and I feel more at ease. It's too bad I will have to say goodbye to all of these people and this castle tomorrow. I think I could learn to enjoy it here, though I would miss my mother. If I were allowed to visit the gardens and the forest outside of the castle, I would be a very happy girl.

An image comes to mind, that of the king, and a shudder goes down my spine. What about him? Could I live in a place where the man in charge is an animal of some sort? Some kind of half-monster creature I'll never understand?

Intrigue takes the place of fear as I realize that's exactly what I would like to do. My whole life, I've been chasing after wild creatures trying to understand them. What could be more thrilling than studying the king, determining how it is that he seems to be half-human, half… something else?

I realize I've lost the conversation again when an older woman a few seats down says something about poor Queen Sophia never getting to see her son marry. Everyone makes a soft, sad noise, and I go along with it a beat too late because I hadn't been paying attention.

No one knows how the king and queen died, only that they passed and their son became king. That was before I moved here, but Fiona told it all in the greatest detail she could. It all happened shortly after the villages between Luna Hollow and Hexeton were claimed--under mysterious circumstances.

When the staff brings out dessert, I don't think I have room for another bite. I've watched the daintiest of women at the table devour plates full of meat and side dishes and don't expect them to have room for chocolate cake either, but everyone says they'll have a slice, so I take one, too.

Before anyone lifts a fork, Ellison says, "Let's salute Bexley on her birthday. While this isn't the same sort of birthday cake I hope you had at home yesterday, I do hope it's delicious." He has a twinkle in his eye that makes me wonder if somehow he does know I had chocolate cake for my birthday yesterday.

Everyone toasts to my health and wishes me a happy birthday. My cheeks go pink as I thank them. I take a bite of cake, and it is delicious. The chocolate melts in my mouth, coating my tongue in sweet, rich flavor, and the cake itself is so moist, it practically dissolves. Someone is going to have to roll me to my room.

After supper, it's Ellison who walks me to my room. Outside of my door, he pauses and asks, "Did you have a nice time?"

I nod. "Yes, everyone was lovely. Thank you."

He smiles at me. "I hope you have sweet dreams." With a bow of his head, he turns to go, but I reach out and grab his arm, afraid this might be the last time I see him. He looks down at my hand and then up into my eyes, expectantly.

"Will I see you tomorrow? That is, will you be the one to take me home?"

I see the hesitation in the flicker of his eyes as he says, "I'm sure you'll see me tomorrow." But that's all he says, and then, he walks away swiftly, leaving me wondering what caused such a reaction. Will someone else be taking me home? Will he possibly miss me, too?

I walk into my room and begin the search for a nightgown. I am exhausted and looking forward to sleeping in such a comfortable-looking bed, but I wonder if my dreams will be full of haunting yellow eyes.

WHAT DO WE DO NOW?

Canaan

I'm sitting in my room, staring at the wall, sipping a glass of wine when the soft knock on my door comes. It's later than usual. Normally, entertaining these women at the evening meal only takes an hour or so, but tonight, it's been nearly two hours since Ellison escorted Bexley away from me.

I shouldn't be too surprised. She is interesting and lovely. Who wouldn't want to speak to her?

"Come in." I take another sip and wait for Ellison, my Beta, to enter the room. He closes the door behind him and slips into the darkness, taking a seat across from me.

It takes him a moment to speak. All he asks is, "Well?"

Normally, he says something like, "We'll try again. Another girl from such-and-such is turning twenty-one the day after tomorrow," but even he knows there's something different with this one.

Of course, that may be due to the fact that I insisted he accompany me to her house earlier this morning. It takes a lot to drag a man who hasn't left his home more than a half a dozen times in seven years out into the real world, especially in broad daylight.

The answer to his question lingers on the back of my tongue. I know what I should say, but I'm not sure I want to tell him. He is my oldest friend. His father was my father's Beta before he was killed in the war. Only a handful of our people had fallen taking the border towns since they had no real leadership to stop us, but Quinton Lake had stepped between my father and a silver bullet, something I will always be thankful to Ellison and his family for.

So, I should be able to tell him the truth. Yet, I don't speak fast enough.

"Canaan," he says, speaking candidly. "If it's her, let me know. It has to be scary, but the Moon Goddess may have finally answered our prayers."

I scoff. Praying is something I did in my youth, but whatever I am now, I can't expect the Moon Goddess or anyone else to have pity on me.

"You're not answering." He leans forward and pours himself a drink in the glass I left out for him. I expect Justin will be in soon. He's our pack healer and my other best friend. Maybe I should just wait for him to join us before I admit the truth.

Stalling, I ask, "What does everyone else think of her?"

"They love her," he assures me. "She's delightful. Most of the women just sit there at dinner in a trance. She actually joined in the conversation some."

A chuckle escapes my throat. "Of course, they are stunned," I remind him. "Who wouldn't be after seeing me? They've just run screaming from a room where they've seen a monster. And we expect them to enjoy a pleasant meal and some jovial conversation."

His eyes narrow slightly as he takes a drink. "She didn't scream, I'll remind you. She's used to being outside where there are plenty of...." He stops talking, noting he's painted himself into a corner.

"Animals?" I ask. "Wild creatures? Monsters?"

"Curiosities." I'm not sure that's any better, but I laugh at his attempt. "She likes to learn about such things. Maybe she would take an academic interest in you."

"Oh, good. Just what every man wants. Someone to poke and prod him to see how he literally ticks."

"Not what I meant," Ellison says dismissively. "I just mean, she's got to be around you and get to know you before… anything else can happen. If she's the one. You still haven't said either way."

There's a second knock on the door, and I'm happy for a short reprieve. Justin joins us, taking the final glass from the table and filling it. He sits in the chair to my left. "She's delightful, Canaan. Everyone thinks so. Naomi is begging me to let her stay, even if she's not the one."

It warms my heart to hear that about my mate, but that's not how this works. If Bexley wasn't the one who could break the spell, I couldn't keep her here. The occupants of the castle are the same people who were here the day the curse was set into place. No one else can come or go—except for my mate.

"I'm a bit concerned," I begin, setting my glass on a coaster on the coffee table. "I don't want everyone to erupt in a tizzy."

They exchange a look before Ellison hazards his question again. "So… Bexley is your mate?"

I let out a deep breath and nod. I see the joyous smiles on their faces, and they both let out a soft laugh filled with glee. "This is exactly what I'm afraid of," I remind them. "The two of you, sitting in my presence, can't manage to keep your happiness in check. What's it going to be like for everyone else? The entire castle will be in an uproar."

"What's wrong with that?" Justin asks me. "It's been years since we've had any reason to celebrate."

"Because," I begin, letting out a sigh, "it just means more disappointment when this doesn't work."

"When it doesn't work?" he repeats, looking from me to Ellison. "Of course, it will work. How could it not work? She's your fated mate, and the witch said—"

"I know what the witch said," I interrupt him. "She said my fated mate had to fall in love with me. It's one thing for me to feel the mate bond with her and quite something else for her to come in blindly and fall for me. May I remind you that Bexley is a human? There's no way she'll be able to feel the pull, which will make it all the harder for me to convince her to give me a chance. Not to mention I'm sure she'll run screaming the moment she sees me in the light of day."

"Not Bex," Ellison says, using a nickname like they are old friends. I'm glad he likes her, but the protective part of me, my wolf, wants to growl at him and warn him not to become too friendly with her. "I'm telling you, she's different. We're still looking into her father. Maybe there's something there."

"She's not a shifter," Justin offers. "I examined the hair sample we lifted, and it appears that she's human at first glance. Of course, she is from Hexeton, so I will need to do some further research."

"If she were a witch, wouldn't she know that?" Ellison asks.

"Not necessarily." I reach for my glass again and take a sip before saying, "If no one taught her about her ancestry, there's a chance her powers are dormant."

"Why wouldn't someone from Hexeton want their offspring to know they have magical powers?" Ellison changes position in his seat.

"Who knows? But it's a possibility I need to check into," Justin says. "I can run those tests, but it will take a while. There's not a lot of witch samples to run comparisons to."

I wish we had something from the horrible woman who stormed into the castle that fateful night and changed our lives forever, but I don't even know her name.

A weariness that begins in my bones rustles through my body, and I yawn. I should go to sleep. It's been a long day for all of us. I hardly slept last night. Though I had no reason at the time to get my hopes up, anticipating meeting Bexley kept my mind up asking questions throughout the night.

"We should let you get some sleep," Justin says.

"She thinks she's going home tomorrow," Ellison chimes in before any of us can get up. "I take it she's not?"

Again, I hesitate. Every part of me says this won't work, and I should just resolve myself to my current state. But then I think of my parents and the misery this spell has cast on the rest of the castle. I have to at least try. "She'll need to stay."

"There's a possibility she might not be able to leave at all until the spell is broken," Justin reminds us. "Should we test that theory out?"

The spell the witch cast was so complicated and overwhelming, there are parts of it I'm not sure I understand. I know I have to meet my mate and have her declare her love to me before I turn twenty-five if I'm to lift the curse, but the other specifications we've simply worked out over the years.

The right answer comes to me quickly, and I shake my head. "No, don't try to take her home. I'm sure she'll find herself making a run for it eventually. Then we'll know."

"She won't," Ellison says.

Justin only laughs.

I pull myself to stand. My legs are sore from the uncomfortable position I must twist myself into in order to sit like a normal man, but I've gotten used to it. "She will," I guarantee him. "And when she does, both of you will be ready to go after her."

With that, I retire to my bedchamber, wondering if I'll dream of Bexley Kessler.

CHANGE OF PLANS

Bexley

The soft, warm embrace of a thousand goose feathers wraps around me. I sigh and stretch, not wanting to leave the most comfortable sleep of my life, but when I open my eyes, I see sunlight peeking through the edge of the curtains, and I know it's time for me to get up.

I take in the beautiful bedroom and smooth down the comfortable satin nightgown I'd found in one of the drawers as I make my way to the attached restroom. This one is so much larger and nicer than my bathroom at home. I could spend hours in the huge bathtub. Unfortunately, I haven't had a chance to try it out, and since I've obviously slept in, I decide to take a shower instead. As much as I am enjoying my time here, I need to get home to Mother.

Despite my best efforts to hurry, I take a long shower using all of the amazing products I find on a shelf within the massive stall. When I'm afraid I'm about to drain the hot water out of the entire castle, I make myself turn the water off and grab a towel. I dry off and put on a robe before stepping back into my bedroom.

Anna is there, bustling about. "Good morning, dear," she says with a cheerful smile. "I was just coming to check on you. Would you like your breakfast in here? I'm afraid everyone else has already eaten. It is half-past ten, after all."

My cheeks flare at the realization that I've slept so late. "That would be lovely, thank you."

"Of course." She presses the button on the wall and speaks into the tube, giving the staff instruction to bring up my breakfast. I imagine whatever the chefs have prepared will be magnificent.

Anna opens the armoire and pulls out a lovely pink day-dress. "What do you think of this one for today, miss?"

"It's beautiful." I sit at the vanity and brush out my damp hair. "But don't you think I should wear my own clothes for the journey back?"

I'm not looking directly at her, but I can see Anna's expression in the mirror. Hesitation takes over before she says, "Uhm, I think this one will look lovely on you. It's yours." She sets the gown on the bed, along with the undergarments I'll need.

Any thoughts I've had of asking her what is troubling her disappear when my food arrives and the scent of bacon and eggs hits my lungs. I can't remember the last time I had a slice of crispy bacon, and my mouth is watering already.

Anna thanks the servant and sets my food on a little table near the window. "I'll leave you to it, dear. After breakfast, I believe Ellison will be in to see you." She smiles, but I see something other than cheerfulness in the curve of her lips.

It looks a bit like pity.

I thank her and finish getting ready for the day, slipping on the dress she laid out for me before I eat my breakfast. While it's a bit boring to eat alone, I take my time and savor every bite.

The curtains are open now, so I can take in the forest. I see several birds fluttering around and a smaller creature I think is either a squirrel or a chipmunk. It's hard to tell from here. I smile, thinking about all of the secrets the forest must contain, but it's a bit disheartening knowing I won't be here to explore them.

The sky is overcast, and I have to wonder if we'll get any snow. It seems fitting that I would leave this cheerful place and return to my home village on a blustery day.

I think of the king. When I first laid eyes on him, sitting in the shadows in his office, it was frightful. But the more I think about it, the more I realize my eyes must've been playing tricks on me. He couldn't possibly be a half-human, half-monster. Maybe he just has long hair and an underbite. Regardless of what he looks like, he is our king, and I should think kindly about him.

I do remember Fiona saying she'd seen him when he was a prince. He used to come to the villages some. She said he was a handsome man with caramel blonde hair and hazel eyes. Unless my mind is playing tricks on me, that's not who I encountered last night.

None of it matters, though. I will be leaving soon, and that means either I'll somehow forget all about it or I'll be pledged to keep what I've witnessed to myself.

I can't imagine how they must convince women not to say anything because this place is so fantastic, but I don't believe in magic either, so that's the only answer that makes any sense. Unless they have some scientific way of making us forget.

I'm finished eating and continue to stare out the window, sipping on a second glass of orange juice, when there's a knock on the door.

It'll take me a moment to get there since this room is so large, so I call, "Yes?" and it opens. Ellison sticks his head in, his curly mop of hair unruly as always. I can't help but smile.

"Good morning, Bex," he says. "Can I come in?"

"Of course."

He leaves the door open a bit, which I assume is because I am an unmarried woman, and this is—for now—my bedchamber, and he is an unmarried man. Ellison is always the gentleman.

With his long legs, he's at my table in a few strides. I offer him a seat, and he takes it. "How was your breakfast?"

"Delicious." I slide the platter closer to the window so it's out of our way. "Did you eat already?" I don't have much in the way of left-overs, but I'd feel rude not to offer him anything.

"I did," he says with a nod. "We missed you at breakfast, but I understand why you might want to sleep in. The beds in the castle are divine, aren't they?"

Giggling like a schoolgirl, I say, "They are." I'm not sure why I'm embarrassed. He sleeps here every night, so he knows how comfortable it is. "Are you here to collect me?" I'm going to miss this place, but I can't wait to see my mother's face.

His disposition shifts. "About that…."

My eyebrows raise as I try to figure out what has brought upon the sudden change. Ellison looks down at his hands, which he is slowly rubbing together. "What's the matter?"

"We, uh, aren't going back to your house today." He lifts his green eyes and stares at me for a moment.

"Oh?" I take a deep breath and swallow down my disappointment. "I thought it was just for one night."

"It is," he says quickly. "I mean… it usually is. But, uhm, you're a little different than some of the other girls. The staff just adores you, as does everyone else in the house, myself included." I think I see his cheeks turn a bit pink at that comment, but he rushes through it. "The king thinks you're quite intelligent and lovely, and he'd like for you to stay a bit longer."

He almost had me convinced with his comments about the staff and the other people who live in the castle. I wasn't much of a conversationalist at supper, but I did enjoy getting to know everyone. I thought Olive and Naomi were nice and could see myself being friends with them, particularly Naomi, who seemed to take an interest in my love for animals.

But the king? There's simply no way that he wants to keep me here. Based on the few seconds I spent in his presence the evening before, how could he possibly? I stumbled through a greeting and then took off like I thought a monster was about to chase me down and eat me for dinner.

"No."

The word leaves my lips before I can even attempt to check it. Ellison raises an eyebrow and looks at me hard. "Come again?"

"I said no," I repeat. "I can't stay here. Not because, as you claim, the king wants me to. Ellison, I belong at home with my mother. While you and everyone else I've met has been kind to me, and I appreciate it, the king didn't even turn the light on in his office for me to see his face. There's no way he wants me to stay here, and if he does, well, it has to be for something nefarious."

"Nefarious?" he repeats, and then he bursts into a rich chuckle that makes me feel silly. My face is on fire. He shakes his head, his curls dancing. "No, Bex. It's nothing like that."

I do rather like this little nickname he has for me, but I can't let it distract me. "Then what does he want me for?"

"To get to know you better," he insists. "King Canaan doesn't let many people into his inner circle, but he's always looking for people he can trust. He didn't turn the light on because he has… a condition, one you may have seen traces of when you encountered him. It's embarrassing for him. Hence, he doesn't go out in public. He's looking for someone who can see past that and get to know him for himself. He thinks you might be that girl, and I concur."

I stare at him, unblinking, for what seems like an eternity going over all of that information in my mind. Ellison concurs? I might be the girl who can get to know the king for himself? Is he implying he thinks I should court the king? It's preposterous. Not only am I the furthest thing from princess material anyone could ever imagine, I'm disappointed that Ellison would so readily hand me over to another man.

I guess the spark I thought I felt with him is nothing more than friendship. He probably flirts with everyone. Still, I've been feeling this tug inside of me since I first met him, and I foolishly thought perhaps he felt it, too.

Now, I just feel embarrassed.

"I don't want to," I say, folding my arms. "I want to go home and see my mother."

He seems exasperated as he blows out a breath. "Not today, Bex."

"Bexley," I correct him. He doesn't get to call me that anymore.

"Sorry. Just…" He shakes his head. "I wish I could make you both happy, but I can't, and my first duty is to the king."

I want to believe that he's telling me the truth, that he cares about my happiness, but now I feel like everything that's happened to me so far today has been nothing but a ridiculous lie. Before I know what I'm saying—again—the words leave my mouth. "I want to see him."

His forehead scrunches. "Who? Garth?"

Bile rises in the back of my throat. "Goodness, no. I never want to see him. Why would you say that?"

"Sorry. I just thought—" He stops and shakes his head again. "Who?"

"The king!" I blurt. Even to my own ear, I sound aggressive. This man is an important noble, and I'm practically shouting in his face. "I would like to have an audience with the king, please."

His mouth moves a bit, but no words come out at first. Eventually, he says, "I'll see what I can do."

Ellison steps out into the hallway, and I take a deep breath wondering what in the world I have gotten myself into? If I get an audience with the king, what am I going to say? And if I don't…. That means I'll be trapped here indefinitely.

AUDIENCE WITH THE KING

Bexley

I FOLLOW ELLISON DOWN THE CORRIDOR TOWARD THE DARK PART OF the castle. He's not holding my arm like he was the night before, and he's walking so fast, I can barely keep up. About half an hour after I made my demands, he left the room and then came back to tell me that King Canaan was willing to meet with me.

Barely breathing, I do my best to tamper down my nerves. My lack of oxygen has little to do with how fast I'm walking and everything to do with seeing the king again. A thrumming in my heart has me undulating between rushing to keep up and slowing down and fading into the walls. Would it be possible for me to ditch Ellison and find the nearest exit? Could I run all the way back home from here? I doubt it, but if the king is as scary today as he was last night, I might not be able to control myself.

We reach the office door, but Ellison doesn't knock on it right away. Instead, he waits for me to reach him and then says, "Are you sure about this, Bexley? You don't have to do this. You can just go back to your room and wait for him to call for you—the way the rest of us do."

I scoff at him, thinking, if it's true that he's an advisor to the king, he probably comes and goes as he pleases. "I'm fine, Ellison," I lie. "It's not a big deal. He's just a person, right? He's not dangerous."

"Not any more dangerous than I am." He has a gleam in his eye that makes me question whether that was a threat or not. "He won't hurt you, if that's what you're asking."

"I just want to hear from his own mouth why I have to stay, that's all."

He blows out a deep breath and knocks on the door.

Canaan's husky voice sends a shiver down my spine. "Come in."

Ellison pushes the door open and gestures for me to enter, but he doesn't escort me in. I hesitate, silently pleading with him to come with me, but I can read his expressions well enough already to know he's not going to do it.

With a sigh, I step inside. Ellison shuts the door with a resounding bang, and I jump.

I'm in the same position as I was the night before. No light pours through the curtains here. It's practically pitch dark, except for the same wall sconces as last time.

"You wanted to see me, Bexley?" His voice sounds almost inviting, but I don't find myself moving. "You can come over. I don't bite."

A hysterical bout of laughter bounces out of my mouth before I clamp it shut with my hands. I see his outline shift slightly and know he's tipped his head to the side to look at me like I am a buffoon. I sound like one.

Knowing this can't get much worse, I decide to trust him and slide toward the chairs I can barely make out across from him. None of Fiona's stories ended with women being eaten by the king, so I assume that he does, in fact, not bite. I feel my way into the seat across from his desk and note I can see him only slightly better this close.

"W-Would it be possible to... to turn on a light?" I practically whisper.

"No."

It's not an ugly response, but it's not particularly friendly either. I take a deep breath. "Okay. Your Majesty…." I clear my throat, not sure what I wanted to say. When I demanded an audience with him, I was angry. I still am to a degree, but I don't know what I meant to say to him. Other than the obvious.

"Bexley?"

A chill shoots down my spine. Something about the way he rasps my name affects me in a way I've never experienced before, and it's not completely unpleasant.

"Uhm… Ellison said I'm meant to stay here a bit longer." I blurt it out. There—I've started the conversation.

"Yes."

It's all he says. He doesn't move, either. As my eyes adjust to the light, I can see more of an outline. Whether it's his hair or the shape of his head, I can't say, but he has lupine characteristics. His hair looks like a wolf's mane, and his nose is long and angular, like a snout.

"Bexley?"

He's said it again, and while I'm still trying to paint a picture of him in my head, I feel that twitch down my spine once more.

"I… want to go home. Please."

Once again, his answer is direct and to the point. "No."

"But—"

"I said no, Bexley. I'm sorry. I really am."

I want to believe that he means that, but it doesn't make sense to me. "All the other girls who've come here only stay one night," I point out.

He barely moves to lift a hand and set it on a folder on his desk. I can't see anything more, but I wonder if it's not information about me. "You're not like other girls."

He's not wrong about that. "I miss my mother."

"I'm sorry. I've been told you are engaged to a man who lives in your village? Weren't you planning to leave your mother to marry him?"

The mention of Garth has bile rising in my throat again. "That's not true," I begin. "Garth just said that because… he's planning something with my stepfather. I never intended to marry him."

"Interesting. Nevertheless, I assume you do plan to marry one day, which means you won't be living at your mother's house for the rest of your life." His tone is full of dismissal, something I don't appreciate.

"Just because I may leave her one day, that doesn't mean I'm ready to leave her now," I remind him.

I think I see a slight rise in one shoulder, but it's hard to say. From what I can tell, his shoulders are slumped, like he's leaning far forward. It reminds me of when a dog stands up to beg and has to lean forward slightly to keep their balance. "Either way, Bexley, I'm sorry, but my hands are tied at the moment. You have to stay here a bit longer."

"Your hands are tied?" Indignation rushes through me as a spiteful laugh leaves my lips. "You're the king."

"That's what they say." He moves his hand again, and now I can see it's actually… a paw. A glint of light hits what should be fingernails, but they are claws.

It's distracting. While I'm trying to carry on a polite conversation with the ruler of this kingdom, I am fully distracted by my brain trying to decipher what I'm looking at. Is he… part wolf?

Shaking my head, I try to clear my thoughts. He can't be part wolf. "Uhm, I just… if you're the king, can't you do whatever you want?"

"No. I'm afraid it doesn't work that way. Believe me, I wish it did." He lets out a sigh that chills me to the core.

Something is wrong with him, that's for certain, and I don't just mean the way he looks. I remember the stories Fiona mentioned, about how handsome he was. But now he's not. What if he has some sort of horrible disease?

His yellow eyes glow softly, and I can tell he truly does wish he could change this, whatever it is. But he can't, and I have no idea why.

I take a deep breath and say, "Fine. I understand that for whatever reason, I can't leave, but you don't want me here either—"

"I didn't say that."

Now, I am even more confused than before. "You said—or at least implied—that you wished you could let me go, didn't you?"

"What I meant to imply is that I don't want to make you unhappy, Bexley Kessler." I can hear a softness in his tone now, and I want to believe him. Why he called me by my full name, I'm not sure, but it wasn't an accident. I have to believe nothing he says is without intention. "But for now, you must stay here. You can explore the woods on this side of the castle fence, but you must not try to climb it. You can write to your mother to let her know you're safe and happy—whether that's the case or not—but you must understand your letters will be read before they go out in order to protect everyone who lives in the castle. As I'm sure you know, I do have enemies, people who would like to expose me as a monster and bring my reign to an end. I can't let that happen, so I have to use the utmost care when dealing with the people outside of the castle walls."

"Your subjects," I remind him.

Again, he lets out a deep breath. "Yes."

"People who haven't seen you for years."

"Well, that is out of my control."

It seems a lot is out of his control for someone who is the king. "What about your representatives?" I ask him. "Why does no one ever see Ellison or… surely you must have other advisors." I mentally scan the people I met the night before. I believe some of them were advisors and nobility.

"It's all quite complicated, Bexley. The last seven years have been hellish. Ellison does visit the villages on the east side of the mountain and keeps the peace with our local rulers there. The areas on the west are not so easily maintained."

I have no idea what the difference between the two parts of the kingdom are, and I've strayed from my initial point anyway. He's been more than cordial in trying to explain the situation to me. The bottom line is, he's saying I must stay, whether I like it or not.

"How long?" I ask, my question just a whisper.

His hair—or is it fur—moves slightly. "A few months."

It's not an actual answer, but it's better than the alternative—forever.

"I want to see you." Again, I can't control the volume of my voice, and the words are barely audible even to me.

Something flickers on the top of his head. Is that an ear? "No."

"I won't be afraid." It's a lie, and we can both taste it. "Ellison said that you're not dangerous."

"Ellison lies just like you do."

"I've only just met you, but I'm not afraid." Why I am insisting on forcing the king to do something he doesn't want to, I'm not sure, but I suppose it's because he's making me stay when I want to go home.

I do want to go home, don't I?

"You should be afraid of me, Bexley Kessler." It's almost a growl, and for a moment, I am scared of him.

But I think he's bluffing. I think there's far more to him than I am ever going to be able to discover while sitting in this room in the darkness. If only I could force him into the light.

A tingling sensation in my hands has me looking down at them. For some reason, I can see them clearly, though I can't even see my knees. They aren't glowing—that would be impossible—but they feel warmer.

"Bexley, I have work to do. Write a letter to your mother. Let her know you're having a good time, you've made friends, and you've been invited to stay. Don't mention anything about my appearance—"

"Or lack thereof," I press.

He groans. "Just tell her you'll be home soon, but not right away. Now, please leave."

Frustrated, I get up and head toward the door. I know he's the king, and he can order me around, but what harm would it do for him to show me what he looks like?

As I reach for the doorknob, I place a hand on the wall to steady myself, and my fingers brush a familiar object.

It's a light switch.

SHEDDING THE LIGHT

I trace Bexley's movement to the door and see what she's about to do. Cursing under my breath, I take preventative measures and scramble through the door behind my desk that leads to another office just as the room is bathed in bright light. Moving quickly is difficult when I've been sitting for so long, but necessity increases my speed, and I just manage to get my tail through the door when she flips the light switch.

Had I underestimated her at all, I'd still be sitting at that desk, and she'd be running from the castle in horror. Thankfully, I've figured out who Bexley is already, and I know never to trust her.

"Where did he go?" I hear her whisper as she takes a few more steps around the office. I silently slip the lock into place and hope she doesn't have some other means of forcing her way into the room.

She doesn't even approach my desk again. I hear her over by the door when it opens. "Bexley!" The lights abruptly turn off as Ellison steps inside. "What in the actual hell are you doing?"

"It was an accident," she claims, and I know she's lying again. It's interesting because one wouldn't take her for a dishonest person, and yet, she's told at least three lies since she entered my office.

She is afraid of me.

But she doesn't want to go home.

Not right away, anyway. I know how interested she is in exploring the forests around the castle. She wants to do that, though it is true that she misses her mother.

I miss mine, too.

Ellison gets her out of my office. I hear the door lock and their footsteps retreating down the hallway. *"Did she see you?"* he asks.

"No," I tell him. *"Why do we still have lightbulbs in here?"*

"So that those of us who know what you look like can have a meeting and be able to see our notes," he reminds me. *"Where am I taking her?"*

"Back to her room. I told her she can explore the grounds but not go over the wall."

"How could she possibly get over the wall?" he scoffs.

"I don't know, but from what I have figured out about Bexley, I think, if anyone could find a way, it would be her."

I end the mind-link and go back to my desk, turning on my lamp. Her file sits there, her picture staring up at me. I trace a claw along her cheek, and that loneliness that sits in my chest starts to grow. Even if I could let her see me, even if I could somehow make her see that we are mates and that she can trust me, she can never love me. Not when I'm trapped like this.

Only if she's able to lift the curse will I be able to touch her, to hold her in my arms, to caress her cheek this way without tearing her soft flesh. It isn't fair—I've done nothing to deserve this.

Yet, that's how it is, and if I've learned anything over the years of being trapped in this body, it's that I can't feel sorry for myself.

A soft rap on the door has me turning the light off. "Yes?"

Anna walks in, slowly navigating her way across the room to my desk. "How are you, dear?"

She was my nanny when I was a child, and we've always had a close relationship. Behind closed doors, she often uses terms of endearment or nicknames. "I'm all right," I lie.

She smiles and reaches across the desk. I don't let most people touch me, but I find myself extending my paw to her. She pats me lovingly, as if it were a hand instead of a twisted, deformed appendage. I can't even dress myself. David and other staff members struggle with my clothing every morning. I eat my meals like a fucking dog. Everything about my life is miserable.

Except for the people I care about. I know I have to break this curse for them. For all of them.

"She's lovely," Anna gushes. "So polite and warm. And smart as a whip. I'd like to show her the library later, if you don't mind."

I shake my head, even though I know she can't see me. "Not until you take down the family portraits."

"Yes, of course," she replies. "We'll make sure she doesn't see those."

I think about my great-grandfather's extensive section on wildlife and find myself agreeing. "Fine. Make sure someone accompanies her. Probably not Ellison."

"May I ask why not?"

A pang of jealousy stabs me in the heart. Ellison is my best friend —and he's also the most charming man I've ever met. Before the curse, I used to watch him convince women to do all kinds of things —unspeakable things. If I was capable of blushing, I would. "Just try to limit the time he spends with her if you can. Let Justin or Naomi show her around when you can't do it yourself."

"All right, Caney." She pats my paw again. "Can I get you anything?"

"A witch?" I joke. "One in a long black gown with a pointy hat who rides a dragon?"

Anna chuckles. "I'm afraid I wouldn't know where to begin to look to find her, and if she did come back, she might make the situation even worse."

"How could it be worse?" I mumble.

"I don't want to find out. What she did to you and your parents is terrible, darling, but we have a way to make amends. Let's focus on that."

I think of my parents and wonder how amends will be made for them. "All right. I shall do my best."

"You should. Honestly, you should try, dear. She's different, this girl. She didn't run and scream like the others. While I understand she's not particularly thrilled at staying, I know she misses her mother, and I have to think perhaps she also objects to losing a bit of her freedom."

"Losing her freedom?" I repeat. "It's not all that bad, is it? You make it sound like I'm chaining her up in the dungeon."

"Well, no, of course it's not that bad," she revises. "But for a girl like her, one who is headstrong and bold, it is a bit of a change, wouldn't you say?"

I shrug, not sure how to answer that. "It can't be helped."

"I know. I will go check on her. But, darling, you do need to consider that she is right in one thing."

"What's that, dare I ask?" I let out a breath and wait.

"You are going to have to let her see you—eventually."

She's right, and I know it. But I am also headstrong and bold. "No."

Anna laughs and gets out of her chair. "She can't fall in love with a man who lives in the shadows." She leaves, closing the door behind her, and I remind the empty room of what she's said wrong.

"I'm not a man. Not anymore."

Knowing that Anna is taking care of Bexley, I try to get some work done, but something else she said plays over and over in my mind.

My parents.

Bexley misses her mother, and I miss mine as well. Abandoning my work for now, I get up and step through the office I'd hidden in, making my way the back way through the adjoining rooms to the vault at the back of the castle. The entrance is hidden in the wall. In the dark, it's even harder to locate, but I don't ever turn the lights on if I can help it.

I find it and press on the correct stone. It moves, and the door opens. Quietly, I slip inside. It's chilly in here, and even my fur can't protect me from the shiver that goes down my spine.

A sconce on either side of the narrow room illuminates the space. There's no reason for me to hide now. With a deep breath, I stand at my mother's feet, looking at her pale face. She hasn't changed a bit in all these years. It's as if time stands still here.

My father's features are the same as well. He looks rested for once, an expression I'd never noticed on his face before that fateful day.

What his intentions were toward Hexeton, I may never be sure, but he didn't deserve this anymore than I deserve my plight, and Mother was innocent in all of this.

Quietly, I say, "I found her. Maybe… maybe things will be different soon." I know they can't hear me, but from time to time, I like to come in and speak to them as if they might somehow hear.

I can't allow myself to cry. I am the king, and I can't show weakness, not even behind closed doors. Knowing if I stay here any longer I will break down, I leave, closing the door and lurking my way back to my office through the shadows. One day, I'd like to feel the sun on my face again, but that day won't be today.

HE DOESN'T LIKE YOU

BEXLEY

ELLISON IS ANGRY AT ME. IT'S CLEAR FROM THE WAY HE MARCHES AWAY from me, leaving me to rush to keep up. If I thought it was difficult to match his strides when we were going to the king's office, it's at least twice as hard now. When we get to the grand staircase, a maid is waiting there for me. "Will you show Miss Kessler to her room, please?"

She bows in compliance, and he turns to walk away.

"Ellison!" I shout after him. He stops but doesn't turn to look at me. "I'm sorry."

Slowly, he turns around, that angry scowl still etched in his face. "Are you? Do you have any idea what you just did?"

"Yes, I do," I tell him. "I should've never—"

"I don't think you have any fucking idea what you did, Bexley."

The woman next to me cowers a bit at his use of such a powerful swear word. I hold my ground. "I just wanted to see him."

"Yeah, I get that," he says, running a hand through his hair. "But he isn't ready for that yet, so you have to wait. Be patient. Do you have any patience in your whole body?"

"You don't even know me!" I shout, getting worked up again.

"Don't I, though?" He storms toward me, and I am inclined to shrink away like the maid, but I don't. With his nose a mere inch from mine, hunched over so he's my height, he says, "Bexley Rose Kessler. Born October 21. Height five foot seven. Weight one hundred eighteen pounds. Mother—Lynn Marie Storm Kessler Moss. Father—Antonio Frederick Kessler."

"You're just spewing facts!" I move even closer to him so that we are practically touching. "That doesn't mean you know me!"

"Oh, I know you, Bexley. I know you better than you know yourself!"

"What the hell is that supposed to mean?"

He doesn't get a chance to answer my question as Naomi comes rushing into the foyer. "What is going on?" she shouts, pushing both of us apart.

Ellison and I glare at one another for a long moment, but neither of us answer. I don't know how to respond, and I guess he doesn't either.

Stepping between us, she puts both of her palms on his massive chest and gives him a shove. "Go. Run it off. I've got this."

He doesn't answer, only turns and walks away, and I find myself unable to hold back the tears.

Naomi wraps an arm around my shoulders. Turning to the maid, she says, "You can go, Bridgette, thank you dear," and then leads me toward the stairs. "It's okay, Bexley."

I want to tell her all of the reasons why it's not okay, but I can't. I just wipe my tears away on the back of my hand, feeling like a small child.

"Sometimes living here is difficult." We walk slowly up the stairs, and I just listen, doing my best not to cry anymore. "I grew up here, but even I get overwhelmed sometimes. There's too many stupid boys."

That gets a chuckle out of me.

"It's true. They can be so pig-headed sometimes. I have no idea what you and Ellison got into it over, but if I had to wager a guess, he's probably wrong." She's so sweet and kind, it makes me glad I've met her.

But she's not right. "It's my fault," I tell her, my voice just a whisper. "I did something stupid. Two stupid things, I guess, and he called me out on it."

"I'm sure whatever you did it wasn't—"

"I flipped on a light switch." I interrupt her.

We are almost to the top of the second set of stairs when she pauses to consider what I've said. I wonder if I'm going to have to explain, but when she says, "Oh," I know she's got it. "Well, yes, that probably wasn't the best decision you've ever made. So did you… see him? The king?"

"No." I swallow back my tears, and we continue walking again, though she's slid her arm down to grasp my hand instead of holding me in a tighter embrace. "He left the room."

She sighs in relief. "That's a good thing, Bexley. While I understand you're curious, and I don't blame you, facing King Canaan can be a lot. You need to get to know him a bit better before you actually see him in the light of day."

I take into consideration what she's saying and suppose she's probably right. A ton of questions flood my head, but I settle on the most obvious one. "You've seen him then?"

"Yes, of course," she says. "I've known him for years. Since before —" she pauses and clears her throat. "Since before he stopped going out. He used to love to visit the villages, you know? We grew up together. He's a wonderful man."

Man. She says he's a man, and yet, I'm not so sure.

We reach the floor where my room is located and head down the hallway. "Don't worry about Ellison. He just needs some time to cool off."

She said he should go for a run, and I suppose that makes sense, that a man as muscular as he is would get some sort of joy out of exercising. "I thought we were friends, but now, I guess he hates me."

Naomi pushes open my bedroom door and follows me inside, closing it behind her. There's a sitting area in the corner with a small couch and two chairs. I drop onto the couch and tuck a throw pillow in my lap. "He doesn't hate you," she assures me. "He's quite fond of you. But you must understand that everything Ellison does is on behalf of the king." She tips her forehead toward me slightly in a pointed look, and I understand what she's saying.

Ellison wasn't flirting with me or trying to charm me on his behalf —he wants me to like him because he wants me to like Canaan. He's the king by proxy. "Oh. Right."

She smiles and sits next to me on the couch. "When we were younger, before I knew that Justin was my mate, I had the biggest crush on Ellison. He's so funny and relatable. Not to mention handsome. But then, when I turned twenty-one and realized that Justin was the one for me, well, I realized that's just how Ellison is. He can't help himself."

I nod, trying to understand everything she's said, though a bit of information doesn't quite make sense to me. Why did she call Justin her mate and not her husband? And what happened when she was twenty-one? Maybe it's just a coincidence that that's the same age I am now and that's when she discovered she loved Justin and not Ellison?

"Anyway," she says, placing a hand on my leg. "What else did you do that you think was a mistake?"

I go over what I said earlier and realize what the other significant error I made was, but in light of what she's just said, I'm not sure it was actually a mistake. "I guess I shouldn't have asked to meet with him, but I wanted a better understanding of why I must stay here longer than the other women."

Her head rocks back and forth slowly. "Did King Canaan answer your questions?"

"Not exactly." I fidget with the fringe on the edge of the pillow. "He said some things are out of his control even as king."

"That's true." Naomi's eyes stare past me at the wall, as if she's lost in thought for a moment. Then she sighs and says, "It's good he was willing to see you, though. Please, give him some time. As I said before, he's a good man. He has a good heart. I'm sure it's frustrating when you can't see who you're speaking to, and you have no idea what he looks like, but that really doesn't matter in the long run, does it? Isn't it what's inside a person's heart that truly counts?"

I'm not sure what to say. Of course, she's absolutely 100 percent right. "I guess I shouldn't let my curiosity make him uncomfortable."

Her smile brightens. "No one can blame you for being curious. Especially when you have made it clear how much it interests you to make observations in the wild. But I assure you, Canaan is a man more than he is anything else, regardless of the impressions you may have gotten from that creepy shadow in the dark." She laughs, though it sounds slightly forced. "My best advice would be to let him come to you. And try not to let Ellison push your buttons, though he really seems to enjoy that." She rolls her eyes.

"Thank you, Naomi. I'm really glad to have met you." I place my hand on top of hers.

"I'm glad to have met you, too. It's nice to have another woman around the castle." She stands and takes a few steps toward the door. "We're all stuck here together, so we have to get along."

"I'm stuck here," I say. "The rest of you can come and go as you please, right?"

Her eyebrows raise slightly before she says, "Uh, right. Yeah, of course. We can." She laughs nervously and then shoots toward the door. I track her with my eyes, waiting until she's gone before I turn around and squeeze the pillow.

Something's not quite right.

Besides the fact that the king seems to be half-something-not-human, some other strange things are going on in this castle. I'd like to know what they are.

But then I recall what King Canaan said to me earlier about exploring. He gave me permission to go outside so long as I don't try to escape. I have no reason to want to do that at the moment. I said I'd stay, so why wouldn't I?

I rifle through the clothes in the armoire until I find something warmer. Most women wear dresses in our kingdom the majority of the time, but it looks to be a little cool outside, so I find some leggings and slip those on under the pink gown Anna chose for me. Then, I pull out a thick cloak and a hat, which I stuff in the pocket for safe-keeping until I'm outside. I wish I had my binoculars, but I don't. Satisfied that I'll stay warm enough, I head out.

As I descend the endless amount of steps, my mind is elsewhere. I'm going over what Naomi said, replaying the parts that don't make that much sense. When I reach the bottom floor, I decide I'll just go right out the front. I have permission after all.

But then I hear voices down a hallway to my left and turn that way instead. I recognize Anna's lilt, and I think she might be talking to David, but I'm not sure because I haven't heard him say much.

I pass a few doors and then stop at an open pair of double doors. Gasping, I step inside and marvel at what I'm looking at. It's a library, and it's the most magnificent place I've ever seen.

LETTERS AND LINGO

Bexley

Books. Thousands of them—maybe hundreds of thousands of them—line the shelves of this magnificent room. It's two stories tall with an endless amount of shelves, some quaint-looking seating areas, and a roaring fireplace. In the distance, I see a wide window with a gorgeous view of what must be the back gardens Ellison was telling me about. I cover my mouth as I stand there and take it all in. Best of all, even from where I'm standing, I can see an area dedicated to zoology.

"Miss Bexley!" Anna calls from across the room. I turn in her direction to see David on a ladder tall enough to reach the highest books, but he's not at a bookshelf. He has a large white sheet in his hand, and he's attempting to drape it over a huge painting on the wall. I scan the room and see two other such paintings already covered. In the distance, another hangs untouched. It's a portrait of an older couple with their arms around one another. They look regal, dressed in fancy clothes with referred expressions on their faces.

"I'm so sorry," I tell Anna as she rushes over to me. "I heard voices and...."

"No, no, it's fine," she says, taking me by the arm and leading me toward the door. "We were just preparing the room for you, that's all. You can't see it yet." Her smile is forced as she tries to lead me away.

Confusion washes over me. "Oh. I will be allowed to use the library eventually, but not now?"

"That's right."

I am almost in the hallway when I hear David yelp and turn back to look at him. The sheet he's attempting to hang has slipped off the far side of the painting, revealing part of a face. Blond hair, one beautiful hazel eye, and part of a strong nose is all I see before she rushes me out of the room.

"Don't you have a letter to be writing, dear?" she asks me.

"The letter to my mother. I completely forgot!" I feel so silly. I've been worried about her, and I'm sure she's been expecting me. "I was just going to explore outside, but I suppose I should do that first, huh?"

"No need to traipse all the way back upstairs, dear. There's a little office right here." She leads me back to one of the rooms I passed and opens the door. The flip of the light switch reveals a small office with a desk and a shelf with supplies. "Why don't you sit right here and write the letter, and I'll make sure it gets out to her later today, all right?"

"Thank you." I study the paper choices on the shelf and settle on a medium weight white piece with the castle's outline embossed on the top in gold. She'll like that. Plucking a pen from the many choices, I sit down at the desk and stare at the paper. What do I say?

Canaan told me not to give away too much information, and I need to respect that. So I decide to keep it simple.

DEAR MOTHER,

I'm doing wonderfully. I hope you are as well. I've made so many friends at the castle that I've accepted King Canaan's invitation to stay a bit longer. I know that may come as a surprise to you, but believe me, it's a good choice. There's an expansive library here and lots of woods for me to explore. I'm excited to see what animals live in the forest.

The king has been a perfect gentleman, so kind and welcoming. I've met a few noble women who are also sweet and a pleasure to speak with. I hope you will be able to meet them someday soon as well.

While I'm not sure when I may be back home, please trust that I am doing well. I will miss you. Please give my love to Fiona.

I will write again soon.

All my love,

Bexley

With a deep breath, I read over it again, satisfied that it doesn't say anything it shouldn't. Then, I choose an envelope from the selection on the shelf. I don't see any red ones, but that's fine. I don't want to alarm her by giving her a reminder of how it was when I left yesterday. I settle on blue and slide the letter inside, but I don't seal it as I remember that King Canaan warned me my letters would be read.

I jot my mother's address on the back of the envelope and am about to leave when there's a knock on the door. "Yes?"

Justin steps inside with a smile. "Hello, Bexley. How are you?"

I wonder how I am meant to answer that. His wife witnessed my argument with Ellison and then spent quite a good amount of time trying to appease me afterward. "I'm fine." That seems like a fitting response. "How are you?"

"Never better," he says, though I think his response is as unfitting as mine is. "Olive and Naomi are sitting down for lunch in the garden terrace. They'd love for you to join them. I'd be happy to escort you."

"Oh." Disappointment settles around me. "I was hoping to go outside to explore. King Canaan said I could."

He nods, and I get the impression he already knows that. "Perhaps you can go after lunch?"

He's right. There's no reason for me to hurry. I'll be here for a couple of months, according to Canaan, maybe longer if what Naomi alluded to is right. "That sounds wonderful."

"Excellent." He strides over to the desk and picks up my letter. "I can get that sent to your mother for you."

"I believe the king wanted to read it first," I remind him.

Justin smiles. "I'm sure he only meant for one of his advisors to read it, but I'll check with him before we send it. This way." He gestures for me to exit the room, so I do, and then he leads me down the hallway in a direction I've never been before.

"This castle is massive," I mutter.

"It is, but you'll learn your way around soon enough." He seems to be a bit older than me, maybe thirty, with kind eyes. I bet he has a lovely bedside manner, unlike most of the physicians I've dealt with over the years.

"Is there any other place I should know to stay away from?" I ask as we walk.

His forehead furrows. "Other than?"

"The library," I reply. "I was in there earlier, and Anna told me it wasn't ready yet."

"Oh. I'm sure that was a misunderstanding."

"They were covering paintings." I haven't allowed myself much time to consider why they were doing that or who that man in the portrait David was covering might be, but it all seems peculiar.

Another item on the list of weird encounters since I've arrived here.

"Some of the paintings in the library portray the former king and queen. Every year, they are touched up. They're probably just preparing for that." He smiles reassuringly, and I nod along, but that makes no sense to me. Why would they cover them up now if they are going to touch them up later?

I decide to let it go. I would like to have the opportunity to look at that painting again, the one of the man with the hazel eyes, but I won't be able to if someone goes back there and takes it down because I sound too curious. "That makes perfect sense," I say with a grin.

"I would only suggest you stay out of the darker parts of the castle. King Canaan likes to be able to move through that space unseen, so if you are there, it will infringe on his privacy, and none of us want to do that. As I'm sure you've gathered, he's very sensitive about his condition." He runs his hand across his chin.

I nod. "Yes, I've got that sorted out. Is he... in pain?" I suddenly realize how awful he must feel being in that form, whatever it is, and the fear I felt earlier is replaced with sympathy.

Dr. Sand arches an eyebrow. "Not usually. Not anymore. He's gotten used to it over the years. But I check on him regularly."

"I'm sure you're a fine physician—and friend." I mean it. I can tell that King Canaan has surrounded himself with the people who care about him most, and that's lovely to realize.

Except it doesn't help me understand what in the world I'm doing here.

We arrive in an atrium full of flowers and plants, and I can't help but pause to take it all in. Justin watches me with a fond, amused expression on his face. "So our zoologist likes botany as well?"

"I do." I reach over to delicately touch the leaf of a plant with large pink flowers. "Unfortunately, I was born with two black thumbs."

"I'm very good with plants," Olive says, stepping over from around a bend in the path. She emerges from behind what I think is a large fern. "Just as my name suggests." She giggles, and I smile back at her. "Perhaps I can teach you a thing or two?"

"That would be wonderful, thank you."

"Of course. Come join us! Naomi is over here as well." She beckons to me, and I move in that direction.

Justin follows, stooping to kiss his wife on the cheek. She's sitting at a little patio table spread with platters of food including little sandwiches and various salads. A pitcher of lemonade reminds me of a warm summer day.

"Ladies, enjoy your lunch," he says as he plucks a sandwich off the platter. Naomi scolds him but we all share a laugh, and then he is gone, and I take a seat, glad to be included.

"You should probably take your cloak off, sweetie," Naomi prompts. "Were you on your way outside?"

I'd forgotten I was even wearing it! Slipping it off, I hang it on the back of my chair. "I was, but it can wait. Thank you for inviting me."

"Of course! You're one of the girls now," Olive says with a wave of her hand. "Dig in."

We fix our plates and chat while we eat. While this meal isn't as meat-heavy as dinner was, I am still shocked and impressed with how much these women can eat. I couldn't keep up with them even if I tried, and I'm not doing the majority of the talking, which should give me more time to eat, but after a couple of small sandwiches, some pasta salad, and some carrots with dressing, I am almost full.

Mostly, they talk about some redecorating Olive is doing in her chambers. I try to chime in and be helpful, but I'm not good at that sort of thing. They do a nice job of asking me questions to include me, though.

"I'm sorry. We're just babbling on," Olive says apologetically. "How has your day been so far?"

I laugh nervously and look at Naomi who only smiles back at me. "Fine, I guess."

"Ellison was being a jerk earlier," Naomi explains.

"Well, it was sort of my fault," I offer. "Although, now that I think about it, he could've been nicer."

"Damn right he could've been," Naomi agrees.

Olive shakes her head and picks up another sandwich. This one looks like chicken salad. "He's such an idiot sometimes. Goddess, I hope he meets his mate soon." She takes a bite and then looks at me wide-eyed, like she's said something she's not supposed to.

I am confused, but I try not to show it. She's said that word again —mate—I assume that's just what people call their spouses here. It's unusual to me, but people from different kingdoms have different lingo, right?

And did she say Goddess instead of goodness? Maybe I misheard her.

"I'm sure he'll find a nice girl sometime soon," I say, and Olive's face relaxes a bit. I look at Naomi. "Justin sure is nice."

"Yes, he is," she agrees with a mischievous twinkle in her eyes. "I wouldn't trade him for anyone in the world."

"What about you, Olive?" I ask. "Do you have a significant other?"

"No." She lets out a sigh. "I'm hoping to meet him soon, though."

Naomi reaches over and squeezes her hand. "I'm sure you will."

I'm praying they don't ask me the same question, but Olive says, "Did you have a boyfriend back home?"

I'm temporarily confused. Does she mean in Hexeton or in Menschen Village? Deciding it doesn't matter, I say, "No. Well, there's this guy who my stepfather wants me to marry, but that's not happening." I can't even think about Garth without wanting to spew all of the lunch I've just eaten on the beautiful pebbled floor beneath my feet.

Olive's forehead crinkles. "Why does your stepfather want you to marry someone you're not meant to?"

Naomi reaches over and taps her arm, and for a moment, it seems like they're having a conversation I can't hear, even though their lips aren't moving.

Olive amends her statement. "I mean, someone you don't have feelings for, of course."

"Oh, well, Garth is wealthy, and a lot of the other women in town are enamored with him. Harvey thinks it would be a good match," I explain.

Both of them shake their heads. "That's ridiculous. You shouldn't marry someone you don't love. Don't you believe in true love or destiny?" Olive asks me.

Taking a deep breath, I consider her words. "I honestly don't know. My parents were very much in love, but I don't really see that with my mother and Harvey. She's happy and comfortable, I suppose, but she doesn't dote on him the way I think my parents did. I don't remember that because I was so young when my father died, but my grandparents spoke of how wonderful and loving their relationship was often."

Now, they are both smiling at me, with dreamy looks in their eyes.

"That's what you want for yourself," Olive surmises. "Don't give up on that." She reaches over and squeezes my arm. "I won't settle for anything less than that, and neither should you."

She's right. I nod in thanks. "Did you grow up at the castle as well?"

Her eyes widen slightly, and she blows out a long breath, shaking her head. "No. I was here visiting when… when… a few years ago. And… I just decided to stay." Tears spring to her eyes, and Naomi reaches over and pats her back.

Once more, I find myself confused, but I don't want to upset her anymore, so I only nod. At least, I'm not the only one who hasn't been here their whole life, I suppose.

"Well, I believe you were on your way outside, weren't you?" Naomi asks me.

"I was." I stand and put on my cloak. "Would anyone like to come along?"

"Oh, no thank you. I think I'll stay in today. It looks like it's about to snow," Olive says.

"I have to go help Justin in the infirmary. I'm a part-time healer—nurse," Naomi explains.

"How wonderful." I ignore her slip and chalk it up to different lingo again.

"You can go through that door right there." Olive takes a few steps over to point to the nearest exit. "Have fun! I hope you see… whatever kinds of animals you hope to see."

"Thank you." I wave at both of them and step out into the cool air, hoping I see whatever kinds of animals I hope to see as well. I have an idea the one with the glowing yellow eyes will not make an appearance today.

MENDING FENCES

"IT'S FINE. YOU CAN SEND IT." I SLIDE BEXLEY'S LETTER BACK INTO THE envelope and hand it to Justin. "How is she doing?"

"She's fine, I think." He changes his position in the chair across from my desk, and I can tell he has more to say. "The girls have slipped up a few times, talking about mates and the like, but Bexley seems to think that's just how we talk here."

"That is how we talk here," I say with a shrug. "As long as no one has mentioned the curse or what she needs to do to break it, I think we're fine."

"I'm certain no one has said that," he assures me. "Although... she did walk into the library as David was covering your portrait. Anna thinks she may have caught a glimpse of it."

"Shit," I mutter, dragging a hand down my face.

"And she certainly saw the one of your parents."

That isn't as bad. The portraits have nothing to do with the curse. I just don't want Bexley to know what I used to look like. I don't want her to think that she's getting to know that man because he doesn't exist anymore. When the curse is lifted, it is my sincere hope that I look as much like my former self as possible, but there are no guarantees. I've been trapped in this wretched body for almost a decade, so there may be no getting back to that, not completely anyway.

And I am most certainly changed on the inside.

No longer the carefree seventeen-year-old prince, I am a hardened, resentful curmudgeon with a chip on his shoulder the size of this castle.

"Where is she now?" I ask, wishing I could see her. It seems ironic that I want so desperately to lay eyes on her when I forbid her from looking at me at all.

"She's outside exploring in the forest to the east of the castle." Justin smiles as he speaks. "So far, she's seen a deer, three squirrels, and a rabbit. The guards are keeping a close eye on her."

"Good." I'm not sure what else to say. I wish I could go out there myself and watch her face light up with each new discovery, but I can't. "See if she needs anything. Binoculars, perhaps."

"Of course." He doesn't move, so I wait, knowing he has more to say. "Do you have a plan, Canaan?"

I shake my furry head. "I do not."

"Don't you think we should come up with one? She can't fall in love with you if she's not with you."

Scoffing, I point out, "She most certainly can't fall in love with me if she is with me."

"That's not true." One corner of his mouth turns down in a pitying look I know too well. "All of us love you—despite having known you your whole life." He's teasing me a bit, but I know his intent.

"I'll try seeing her every day for a bit, see if that makes a difference," I suggest. "Beyond that, I don't know."

"May I suggest you consult with the ladies? Olive and Naomi are both very good at knowing what women want."

It's not a bad idea. "I'll speak to them," I assure him. Ordinarily, I'd like to handle something like this my own way, but everyone's fate depends on how I handle this situation, and we are running out of time.

With that, Justin gets up and heads toward the door. I wait for him to leave before leaning back in my chair. The pain in my legs is unbearable at the moment. I have to get up and stretch. Even though he's our chief healer, I try not to burden him with my problems. He's never seen anything like me either, and it's simply not fair for me to occupy the majority of his time trying to fix me when I am unfixable.

I hobble to the window that looks out on the east side of the castle. I don't usually look outside. It reminds me of everything I'm missing. But this is different. I want to see her if I can.

Pulling back the edge of the curtain, I look outside, hoping to catch a glimpse of her. Lucky for me, she's making her way across the expansive yard back toward the castle. Even though she's far away, my heart feels lighter just looking at her. I can't make out the details, but her form is enough. A genuine smile lights my face for the first time in a long time. I drop the curtain and go back to my desk, and I can't help but pick up the file with her picture on it. Bexley is a beauty, that's for certain.

I can't begin to know if this is going to work or not, if I'm going to be able to make her mine, but if I'm able to, I have a feeling it won't just be the end of this horrible curse that will have us all rejoicing. I'll appreciate every moment I have her in my arms.

Bexley

My time in the woods is quite productive. I see a number of animals and have the opportunity to study a family of squirrels inter-acting. While I got the sensation that I was being watched wherever I went, I never caught sight of anyone out in the woods with me. Once, I thought I heard another crunching noise behind me and turned to see if perhaps Canaan had decided to come out after all, but nothing was there. Nothing I could see through the trees anyway.

As I make my way back toward the castle, a light snow begins to fall. I lift my face to the sky, savoring the feeling of each flake kissing my cheeks. There's something magical about the first snow of winter —even if I don't believe in magic.

I open my eyes and gasp at the form looking down at me from a window in the back of the castle, near the very top. He's difficult to see at this distance, but I can clearly make out glowing yellow eyes. That's about all, except for what appears to be the outline of his head. It does appear to be quite wolf-like, with lots of fur. I'm intrigued but also happy to see him for reasons I can't explain.

He closes the curtain, but my smile lingers as I make my way to the nearest entry way. I open the door, hoping to see a servant nearby that can direct me to my room, but the hallway is unusually quiet for such a large castle full of so many people.

I decide to try to find my way by myself and turn to the left, thinking that has to be the front of the castle. That leads me to a dead end, so I go the other way and end up walking into a place where the lights are dim. Remembering what Justin told me about giving the king his privacy, I quickly turn around and head the other direction.

Trying a few more hallways leads me further into the castle, but I still can't find a path that will take me to the foyer and the stairwell. I find another staircase and ponder going up there, but then, I think I might end up in a turret or something. I determine that's not a good idea and turn around once more.

I'm about to give up and start yelling for help when I turn a corner and see a large form coming toward me. Sighing, I consider rushing away in the other direction, even if it means losing my chance at help.

"There you are," Ellison says with a grin on his handsome face, as if we didn't almost rip each other's throats out not three hours ago. "Are you lost?"

"Yes." I want to be nice because that's how my mother raised me, but I'm also still angry at him. I feel like his entire demeanor has been a lie, and I don't want to fall for him again.

"I can show you how to get back to the front of the castle and the stairs," he offers.

"Fine."

"Bex." He holds his hands out to his side, his head tipped, that smile still in place. "Come on, girl. We had a disagreement. That happens sometimes."

"A disagreement?" I repeat, then I shake my head. "You were right about some of what happened, I'll give you that. But you… haven't been honest with me either." There. I've said enough.

"Wow. A woman who can admit it when she's wrong. I knew I liked you. Come on."

Reluctantly, I fall into step behind him, hoping we can just leave it at that.

We can't.

"Tell me more about how I was right."

I growl, and he laughs. "I shouldn't have turned on the light. I already admitted that to you. But no harm was done."

"Only because the king's faster and smarter than you give him credit for," he replies. "Whatever it is you think I've lied to you about, Bex, I assure you, I'm just doing my job."

"I know." I want to say more, to tell him to stop being such a flirt, but if I do that, I'll have to admit I fell for it, and I'm not ready to admit that either. I probably won't ever be.

He asks me some questions about the animals I saw, and I tell him about them. By the time we reach the staircase, it's like nothing ever happened.

Ellison offers me his hand. "Friends?"

I take a deep breath and wonder if I can trust anyone under this roof. Seeing as though I have no choice, I shake his hand. "Friends."

He flashes me that cheesy smile, and I head up the stairs, deciding now is as good a time as ever to try out that bathtub.

WE HAVE TO DO SOMETHING

Canaan

Several days have passed since Bexley first arrived at the castle. I've been trying to talk myself into visiting with her, but it's been too difficult. The more time that slips away, the more desperate the situation becomes. Finally, I decide I have to bite the bullet and do something. She can't get to know me if I never see her, and while Ellison and the others tell me she asks about me, I haven't seen her in person in far too long. It's time to remedy that, so I've called in the experts.

"Ask her questions, but don't be too nosy," Olive suggests. "Take an interest in her, but don't pry."

"And compliment her," Naomi offers. "But make sure it sounds genuine."

"Don't mention her boobs, though. No girl wants to hear a guy thinks she has nice tits. It just makes us feel like meat," Olive insists.

"I would never—" I begin, but then I decide it's better to just nod along. "Fine. What about a gift?"

"Get her a gift based on something you know she likes, like a special interest." Naomi seems excited now. "Like animals!"

"The binoculars!" Olive claps her hands. "Get her the best pair of binoculars."

"It's not as if I can just go to the store," I remind them. While the curse does allow us to leave the castle for a few hours without making us horribly ill, I'm not traipsing into the village to peruse the binocular selection looking like this.

The women exchange a look before Naomi says, "We could go."

"I have a better idea." It suddenly occurs to me that my father used to have a very nice, expensive pair of binoculars that he obviously isn't using anymore. I can get to his office without anyone seeing me. "I'll handle it. Anything else?"

"Flowers?" Naomi rubs her chin. "Do you know what her favorite color is?"

"You can't go wrong with pink roses." Olive chimes in. "I can cut some and bring them. I've got some in the atrium."

"Perfect. Thank you." I take a deep breath. Back before the curse, speaking to women was one of my specialties. I was a very good flirt, a lot like Ellison, though I was a lot more sincere. At least, I hope I was. Now, all of my imperfections keep bubbling to the surface, and I know she's going to run screaming from me the moment I turn on my desk lamp.

Sensing my apprehension, Naomi stands and walks around the desk. When she wraps her arms around me, she doesn't cringe away from my fur or my twisted bones. "It'll be fine, Canaan."

"Thank you." I wish I could hug her back, but I might accidentally claw her. "I appreciate you both so much."

Olive smiles and stands, but she doesn't approach, and that's okay. The daughter of a noble from a kingdom on the other side of our western border, Olive was just here at the wrong time and got caught up in all of this. We didn't grow up together, so we're not as close, and she should honestly resent me for ruining her life. I'm lucky she is so kind and helpful.

I want to bang my head on the desk after they leave, but I don't. Instead, I head through the darkened hallways to my father's office. It's been closed up for a while. When I open the door, a distinct musty smell greets me. I decide to keep my head down as I cross the room to his desk. On the walls are a ton of family portraits—including plenty of me growing up. I don't really need to see my carefree, smiling face at the moment.

In his desk, third drawer down on the right, I find the binoculars. They're in perfect shape and look expensive—which they are. I hope she likes them. I think he would approve of me letting her have them since he hardly used them anyway.

Slipping them into my pocket, I turn to go and catch a glimpse of the portrait of my family on the wall near the door. My mother's beauty takes my breath away. Her long hair is perfectly curled to frame her face, her blue eyes twinkling. Father looks regal, his facial hair nicely trimmed, and his hazel eyes, the same shade mine used to be, are warm and sincere.

And then there's me.

I had to have been about fifteen in the photo. In my mind, life was just starting. I had just begun to gain some independence and start my own adventures. I dreamt of finding my fated mate, marrying her, and taking over for my father in a few decades. I had no idea the horror that was right around the corner.

A groan escapes my lips, along with some drool, another horrible side effect of this curse. I wipe it on the back of my sleeve and head back to my office.

As I'm making my way through the back tunnels, I get a mind-link message that Olive and Naomi have set everything up in the sitting room near my office. *"It's plenty dark enough in there,"* Olive assures me. *"And we put the lamp from your desk on the table so you will still have the same amount of light to reveal yourself in a cozier setting."*

I'm not sure what to say. I'm much more comfortable in my office, but I do understand their thinking. I say, *"Thank you,"* and then take a deep breath and add the inevitable phrase I've been avoiding. *"Send her in."*

I make it to the sitting room and survey the situation. They're right—it is dark in here. I can make out the table and two chairs in the corner. I hobble over and see a huge vase of flowers, as well as a plate of cookies and two glasses of lemonade, with straws. The pitcher sits on a sideboard. Obviously, I won't be eating any cookies in front of Bexley. That would be a disaster. But it was a nice touch. I have good friends.

I reposition the chairs slightly so mine is more in the shadows and hers is as far away from me as possible without sitting her across the room and then take my seat, adjusting my posture a few dozen times before finally giving up. There's no way to look distinguished when you're a monster.

A light knock on the door has me jumping in my seat. I've gone from being a confident warrior to a sniffling coward. "Come in," I call, my voice cracking.

Bexley pokes her head in and looks around, confused.

"Over here."

She turns her head in my direction, and I think I see a smile, but it's dark, and that doesn't compute. Why would she be happy to see me?

"Your Majesty!" She strides across the room not fearing me or the dark. "It's great to see you. How have you been?"

Why does she sound like she really means that? Her tone is warm and inviting, like we are old friends who haven't seen one another in some time instead of perfect strangers or prisoner and captor.

"I've been well," I lie. "Please, have a seat."

She pulls out the chair across from me and has a seat. "Are these roses?"

"Yes." I clear my throat. Why do I sound so timid? "They're from the atrium. I hope you like them. They're pink." Goddess, I sound so fucking stupid.

Inhaling deeply, Bexley sticks her nose close to the flowers and breathes them in, and I feel a twitch low in my body I haven't felt in years. "Lovely. Thank you. I'm so glad you wanted to see me. I've been here for a while now, and we haven't had a chance to speak."

"I'm sorry. I've been very busy," I lie. "How has it been?"

"Wonderful. I've been exploring a lot outside, and the library is fascinating. Did you know you have one hundred eighty-three books on zoology?"

I chuckle. "I hadn't counted them, but I knew there were a lot."

"A lot of them are about wolves." She sounds puzzled as to why that would be. "I haven't actually seen a wolf yet, but I've seen tracks. Oh, and I believe there's a family of foxes living in a hollowed out log near the fence by that little brook. Do you know where I mean? On the east side of the castle grounds."

"I'm not sure. I'll have to go check it out." I'm trying to make polite conversation.

So when she says, "I can show you!" I balk.

"Perhaps." I can't imagine walking around outside in broad daylight with her.

"I'm sorry. You probably invited me here for a specific reason, and I'm rambling on about animals."

"No, I just wanted to speak to you." That's not entirely true. I am supposed to do more. I am supposed to show her what I look like, but maybe I don't have to do that today. Maybe I can stall. "Would you like a cookie? Or some lemonade?"

"These smell delicious." She takes a cookie, sets it on her plate, and snaps off a bite. I have to look away as she slides it into her mouth, her perfect pink tongue darting out to lick her lips. The mate call is so strong on my end, and she can't feel it at all. It's hardly fair. "So good!"

"I bet they are." I move slightly in my chair, readjusting.

"Would you like one?" She lifts the tray slightly in my direction.

"No, thank you."

She sets it down and takes a sip of her lemonade. "Everyone here has been so nice."

"I'm glad to hear it. And your mother? Have the two of you been corresponding?"

"We have been." She swallows a bit more cookie before continuing. "I miss her, of course, and I know she misses me, but she understands that it's necessary for me to stay here a bit longer. She doesn't know why, of course, and neither do I."

That's a question, one I can't answer, not at the moment, anyway.

Instead, I change the subject. "Oh, I have something for you." I pull the binoculars out of my pocket and set them down in front of me, no easy task with my mangled paws. Then, I give them a push in her direction so she can't see my hideous hand. "I know you can't truly see them now, but those are a pair of binoculars. I think you'll find them useful."

"Binoculars?" She scoops them up and holds them close to her face, trying to get a look at them. The horrific idea that she might try to use them to see me better crosses my mind, so I'm relieved when she doesn't open them. "Thank you so much, Your Majesty. These will come in so handy. I think there's an owl in one of the trees that's actually been coming out in the daytime for some reason. I'd love to get a better look at him."

"You're welcome, and please, call me Canaan."

She looks up at me, the binoculars momentarily forgotten. "Canaan?" Her eyes are wide. "Don't you think that's a bit informal, sir?"

I shrug. "You're a guest in my home. You have been for some time, and you shall be for... longer. Besides, Bexley, you are important to me for reasons you can't comprehend at the moment." I have been far more honest with her than I probably should've been, but the sincerity of it feels good pouring out of me.

She places the binoculars on the table and folds her hands in front of her. "I'd like to see you."

"I know..."

"I can promise you, Your—Canaan, that whatever this condition is that you have, I won't be frightened or judgmental. I've gathered a bit of information from my discussion with the others in the castle since I've been here, and while I'm not certain of the details, I know that whatever afflicts you is out of your control. Justin is doing all he can to remedy it, I'm sure. But... I am a scientist, at least, I like to think of myself as such. I obviously don't wish to examine you as if you were a wild creature, but my study of animals allows me a deeper understanding than most."

When she finishes speaking, she bobs her head slightly, and I get the impression she's been practicing that speech for a while, probably since the last time we met, and I denied her request to turn the light on—and she did it anyway.

I contemplate her request. That is, of course, the reason why I called her here in the first place, to see me. That and I wanted to see her. Whenever she is far away, even on the other side of the castle, I feel a tug on my heart. I can't imagine what would happen if she were to leave. I'm afraid it might kill me. So seeing her has to be a priority for me, even if it's uncomfortable–for both of us.

I take a deep breath and begin the speech I have prepared. "Bexley, you have to be prepared for what you will see if I decide to turn the light on. My appearance is gruesome at best. Every other woman who's entered my office and seen my silhouette has taken off running in terror."

"I didn't," she reminds me.

"No, you didn't. I remember, and I appreciate that. But… you must know that with the lights on, even this small lamp, you'll be able to see how hideous I truly am."

She's shaking her head as if she can't believe it, so I feel compelled to describe myself.

"Have you ever read those children's books, meant to horrify young people not to go into the woods at night, that talk about werewolves?"

"Yes." She sits up straight in her chair, leaning in.

I nod. "Well, imagine something like one of those beasts—the long snout, pointy fangs, enormous tongue that doesn't quite fit, uncontrollable slobbering, mangy fur, and these evil-looking, unholy eyes. Imagine being caught somewhere between that wolf-like creature and a human. Mangled, twisted bones set at strange angles with patches of skin and tufts of fur." I shake my head, my stomach turning just thinking about it. No, I can't allow her to see me.

Bexley isn't leaning away from me. She doesn't get up and dart out the door. Instead, she reaches a hand across the table. My paw lies within her reach. I want to pull it away, but I don't.

Her fingers trace lightly over what should be fingers. Instead, they are some variation of toes with enormous claws on them, turned inward so that they are practically useless. She runs her hand over the tufts of fur and up what should be my hand to my wrist. With her palm lying flat on top of the back of my paw, she says, "I'm not afraid of you, Canaan. You've given me no reason to be. Everyone here says how kind and benevolent you are. They are all such good friends to you. I should like to be your friend, too."

With her leaning across the table, she's closer than she has ever been before. I take a deep breath, close my eyes, and turn on the lamp.

BREATHLESS

Bexley

WARM LIGHT BATHES CANAAN'S FORM AS HE TURNS ON THE LIGHT NEXT to us. I don't make a sound. Not a gasp. Not a whimper. Not a sigh. Nothing.

I've prepared myself for this moment. Over the last several days as I've explored the castle and spoken to his staff and friends, I've gotten an idea of what he looks like now.

The portrait in the library? The handsome man I've been hoping to see in my dreams? That's what he used to look like. I only got a glimpse of that painting, but I know that was him.

This is him now.

His description of himself is pretty spot on, though I don't see any slobber, and his tongue isn't hanging out of his mouth as I expected it to be. He does appear to be caught in a transformation. His shoulders aren't even, like his spine is twisted, with one higher than the other. His fur isn't patchy that I can see. It's a lovely gold color, similar to the hair I saw in the painting. He does have large fangs that don't fit inside his mouth when it's closed, as it is now, and he has a long pointy snout like a wolf, but it's also crooked. His ears are offset and jagged, like something has been chewing on them.

I am fascinated.

And yet, I don't want to make him feel like a spectacle either. I'm not here to analyze him. I would love to know how this happened. I've never heard of any disease that can make a person turn into an animal, but then, I'm young and haven't traveled that much. Perhaps there are aspects of this world I have yet to experience.

Slowly, he opens his eyes. I haven't moved. Now, I smile at him, and his eyebrows, or what should be eyebrows in a person, lift. Then, he smiles at me, and something sparks deep inside of me, a small pull I have only felt a few times before—and all of them have had to do with Canaan. I felt it in his office for the first time. I felt it when I arrived at the castle. This time, it's more intense. It's as if my soul knows I belong here—with him.

It doesn't make any sense to me, but I can't deny it or push it away.

I take a deep breath and ask him, "Could I… touch you?"

His bushy eyebrows furrow. "You are touching me."

Giggling, I say, "No, I mean… can I come closer?"

He pulls back, his shoulders pressed against the chair, but his hand is still beneath mine. "I, uh… why?"

"If you're uncomfortable, I don't have to. I just want you to know that I'm not afraid of you. You don't make me uncomfortable."

We sit there for a long moment with my hand on top of his before he finally says, "Okay."

This must be difficult for him. He walks around his own home in the shadows so that he doesn't "bother" his staff and his loyal friends who have stayed here with him despite his affliction. I'm certain now that he doesn't have to do that. While it's true he would most definitely frighten someone if they were to run into him on the streets unexpectedly, these people all care deeply for him. I think he should be able to feel free in his own home.

I withdraw my hand and walk around the table, carefully. He scoots his chair back and looks up at me, sucking in a deep breath. He's waiting for me to take off running. I can sense it. But I won't.

First, I run my hand along the side of his face. He closes his eyes and lets out that breath. I can see some resemblance to the man in the painting, but it's faint. I place my hand on his shoulder, feeling how deformed he is beneath his suit jacket. It's clear he's covered in fur beneath his clothing as well. I run my hand down his chest to his abdomen and then stop. I'm not sure what's gotten into me, but my body is singing, and the lyrics say that I belong here—with him.

Canaan opens his eyes to slits and peers up at me, as if he can't quite figure out what I'm doing. I don't know either, so I wrap my arms around his shoulders and bury my face in his neck. When he places his arms around me, I feel safe. I feel like this is where I'm meant to be. Like this is my home.

"Bexley?" His raspy voice is just a whisper near my ear. "Thank you."

I sit up, feeling my face flush. A thousand thoughts collide in my mind as I try to sort through what's happening. A tingling sensation in my hands has me placing them behind my back. "Thank you." I force a smile, despite the fact that I'm growing more embarrassed by the moment. "I should go."

He nods. "Please, take the flowers and the binoculars with you. Do you want the cookies? They're for you, too."

"Oh, I'm not sure I can carry all of that, but thank you." I take the lovely pair of binoculars that I can now see are blue and trimmed in gold and slip them into the pocket of my dress. The vase is a bit heavy, so I hoist it onto my hip. Before I go, I turn and look at him again. He smiles and then turns off the light. I want to tell him he doesn't have to do that, but the words get trapped on my tongue.

I turn and leave the room, forcing myself to walk at a normal pace so he doesn't think I'm running away from him.

Out in the hallway, I take a deep breath and lean against the wall for a moment. What in the hell is the matter with me? What if he thinks I'm throwing myself at him because I want to be the queen? Is it utterly ridiculous that I could be physically attracted to him when he's—

When he's what? He's a man. He's my king. And he's a kind soul.

It's not his fault he has some sort of an affliction. I wonder if Justin has tried shaving the fur. Would hair grow back?

"Bexley? Are you okay?"

Naomi's voice brings me out of my thoughts. I push off the wall and smile at her. "Yes, I'm fine."

She doesn't seem to believe me. One side of her mouth turns down in a sympathetic half-smile. "I know it's quite a shock when you see him for the first time, but you don't need to be afraid of him."

I stare at her for a moment, not sure how to respond. My reaction to him wasn't fearful at all—and that's potentially more problematic than it would've been if I'd left the room in a panic. Deciding I can't really tell her I have an unnatural attraction to the king, I decide to stick with my original story. "I know. I really am fine." Isn't that enough?

She nods and leads me down the hall toward my room. "Hopefully, you'll be seeing a lot more of him now."

"I hope so, too."

Naomi nods solemnly, like she doesn't believe I mean that. But I do.

I really do.

Canaan

I can't breathe.

Not fully, anyway. I do my best to fill my lungs, but I feel like it's not quite working, like I've been running for several hours and just need to stop, only I haven't ran like that since before the curse, and I'm still sitting in a chair.

But the feel of Bexley's warm hand tracing my body lingers on my fur, seeping into my skin beneath it, into my bones, like she's part of me now.

"What the fuck?" I mumble, but not in a bad way. It was almost as if she could feel it, too.

Like maybe the mate bond somehow reached her, despite the fact that she's human.

Is she, though?

Justin hasn't given me the results of his testing yet, but as Bexley pulled her hand away from me, I swear I saw a slight glow to her hands. It could've been a trick of the light. But the way she hid her hands behind her back afterward makes me think something strange was happening.

There's a knock on the door I recognize to be Olive's. "Come in."

She steps inside. I don't move. I'm still facing the way I was when Bexley was in the room, which probably looks strange to her, if she can see me. I did manage to turn off the lamp.

"How did it go?" I hear the hopeful tone in her voice.

I'm not sure how to answer that. I expected Bexley to either run away in fear or treat me like one of her creatures from the forest. She'd done neither. She'd treated me like I'm a man. For the first time in seven years, I felt like a human.

"It went well," I say, not turning to look at her. My heart is still pounding, and my cock is still slightly stiff. I do have basic animalistic needs, so that's not entirely new, but this time, it had a legitimate reason for making its presence known. It wants Bexley as much as I do.

Unfortunately, that's not something I'm willing to even consider in this twisted form. Apparently, my dick didn't get the memo.

"Oh, good. I knew it would." She clasps her hand together and does some little dance move that makes me laugh. "Do you think you'll be spending more time with her?"

"I hope so." It's a double-edged sword because I need to get to know her better if she's got any chance at breaking this curse, but I also can't constantly respond to her the way that I have today.

Olive takes a cookie from the platter and bites into it. "This is all so wonderful." She practically squeals. "It's happening. It's finally happening! Soon, I'll be able to go home."

She's so excited, I want to do everything I can to make that true for her. But, my fear of failure is too intense for me to do anything more than nod. What if I fail her? What if I fail all of them? I hope she's right, but Bexley is so sweet, so intelligent, so beautiful. It's hard to imagine her choosing to be with me.

Why would anyone want to be with a monster?

DREAMING OF HIM

BEXLEY

THE CASTLE BALLROOM HAS AN ETHEREAL GLOW TO IT. SHIMMERY AND clouded with a blanket of mist, I step into the center of the floor, my long blue ball gown billowing around me. The faces of the crowd around me are obscured by the mist. They don't quite come into focus, but that's okay. None of them are important. I hear their cheers above the sound of the orchestra playing in the corner, which I cannot see. It's all so wispy and dreamlike. I feel like I'm floating on air.

A man steps through the crowd, his face the only one I can see. His smile is genuine, his hazel eyes twinkling in the sparkling candlelight. He's unbelievably handsome with his blonde hair tied back and a dazzling smile. His royal blue suit is fitted, showing off his rippling biceps as he extends a hand to me.

I slip my fingers into his, and he pulls me close, and I can feel his heart beating beneath my palm as we begin to dance. "You're so beautiful." His breath caresses my cheek as he whispers in my ear.

"You're the most handsome man in all the land," I reply, pressing myself

closer to him. He spins me around the ballroom in perfect time to the music. Like everything else he does, he is an excellent dancer.

We continue to dance for an endless time, but then, we are no longer in the ballroom. Instead, we are in a bedroom—our bedroom. The details blend into the background as he lays me down gently on the bed, his mouth covering mine in a heated kiss.

I slip my leg from beneath him so that it's pressed against his hip, pulling him against me. An ache forms deep inside my abdomen, splintering down to my core creating a need that has me arching my back and lifting off the mattress. I need him inside of me.

He knows exactly what I need as he undresses me, planting warm kisses along my neck, down my shoulder and then down to my bare breasts. The clothes come off easily, as if they've magically disappeared, and I don't question it. One thing I've learned since I came to be his is that magic does exist, and it has the power to change everything.

I feel his thick cock pressed against my entrance and lift my mouth to his ear, running my tongue along his lobe before biting down gently. "Please," I whisper. "I can't wait any longer."

He smiles down at me and brushes my hair away from my face, his palm warm on my cheek. "I love you so much, Bexley."

"I love you, too."

I close my eyes as he presses inside of me, filling me completely. Gasping, I stretch to adjust to him, and then, as he begins to move his hips, I rise to meet him, running my hands over the planes of muscle that make up his sculpted back.

He takes a nipple between his lips and sucks, sending a wave of pleasure through me. I thread my fingers through his hair to hold him there as I throw back my head and moan. "Yes, that feels so good!"

He licks and sucks some more while his dick continues to pump in and out of me. I feel myself tightening around him and hold on as my body breaks into spasm. "Yes, Goddess, Canaan, yes!"

MY EYES FLY OPEN, AND I LOOK AROUND THE ROOM. MY ROOM. AT THE castle. This is my bed—and I am in it alone.

Letting out a long breath, I drag my hand down my face. My body aches in places I've never used for their intended purpose. How I know what it feels like to have sex, I'm not sure. Maybe I don't. But if it's even half that good…. Well, maybe one day I'll find out.

I sit up and look around, half expecting the king to be sitting here watching me, laughing at me. I don't think I actually cried out in my sleep, but this dream was so intense, it's quite possible.

It's not the first time I've dreamt of him.

Ever since that day a few weeks ago when he revealed himself to me, I've been having similar dreams. We are often at a ball to begin with, though sometimes we are out in the forest, and then we are in bed, or at least, we are having sex. Sometimes we do it right in the middle of the woods.

Still flustered, I get out of bed and haul myself to the shower. I can't keep thinking about him this way. As much as I would love for his disease to be cured so he can return to his previous form, that's not reality, and I don't even know if it's possible for him to have sex in his present state. It's not like we've discussed it.

Since that first time he turned the light on, we've been spending some time together. We often sit in his office and chat, but sometimes we meet in the sitting room. I've invited him to come out into the woods with me, but he isn't comfortable with that. He's admitted it's because he's self-conscious and doesn't want me to see him in direct sunlight yet. He says he's working up to it, and maybe someday soon he'll be ready.

Once I'm dressed and ready, I wander downstairs and am happy to find Olive and Naomi having breakfast still. Sometimes, I sleep too long and miss it. Today, they greet me and wave me over to the table. "How did you sleep?" Naomi asks.

So far, I've managed to hide my erotic dreams from my friends. At least, I don't think they suspect anything. "Good," I tell them, sitting down and spooning some eggs onto my plate before taking a few slices of bacon as well.

"That's good," Olive says, but I can tell both of them seem a little distracted.

"Is everything all right?" I ask, taking a bite of bacon.

They exchange a glance before Naomi says, "I'm sure it's nothing. We've just been hearing some rumors of unrest in some of the villages, particularly Menschen Village. Have you heard anything?"

I shake my head, worry settling into my stomach, along with the bit of breakfast I've eaten. "No, Mother hasn't said anything in her letters. I can ask."

"Oh, no. You don't need to do that," Olive assures me, rubbing the back of her neck. "It's probably nothing." She forces a smile, but it doesn't hide the worry.

"What sort of unrest?" I ask, trying to seem like none of this is affecting me so maybe they'll tell me more. I pour myself a glass of juice without looking at them.

"Just that people are beginning to grow weary of not seeing anyone from the castle," Naomi supplies. "Namely the prince. And a few people are worried about you."

I set the pitcher down abruptly. "Worried about me?"

She shrugs. "It's mostly localized. Again, it's probably nothing."

I take a sip of my juice. "Garth." He's the only one who can be responsible for this.

"Ellison is going to meet with the villagers today to talk to them, to assure them that you're fine," Naomi tells me.

"I should go, too."

"No!" they both practically shout at the same time.

I startle and scoot back in my chair.

"You don't need to do that." Olive forces a chuckle. "He'll be fine."

Something isn't right. They're still keeping secrets from me. Even though I know what Canaan looks like now, there's more to what's happening here. I can feel it in my gut. "Maybe I should talk to the king about it when I meet with him later."

"You could." Naomi shrugs like it's not a big deal. "By the way, he said he'd like to meet you outside. In the back garden."

My eyebrows raise at what she's telling me. "Really?" I've yet to go out there, and I've never seen Canaan outside before. My heart thrums in my chest at the prospect of a new adventure—with him.

"It's beautiful in the snow." Olive smiles. She's been trying to teach me a bit about the flowers in the atrium, but I am still terrible at gardening. "Lots of flowers still bloom even in the winter."

"All right." I finish my breakfast while they chat about this, that, and the other, and pretend that I have forgotten about going with Ellison, but the thought hasn't gone away. I decide to ask Canaan about it.

Maybe he'll let me go. I might be the only one who can fix things and bring peace to the kingdom again.

MAGICAL TOUCH

BEXLEY

AFTER BREAKFAST, I GO BACK TO MY ROOM FOR A WARM CLOAK AND mittens. I decide against wearing a hat, even though I know I'll be colder without it. I don't want to look silly in front of the king.

Anna is at my door as I bound out. She smiles and says, "I thought maybe it would be helpful if I show you to the gardens, dear."

"That would be wonderful."

We walk down the same staircase as usual and down the hallways I'm familiar with until we are almost at the atrium, and then she turns a different direction down a path I've never explored . As we go, we chat. She asks about my mother, and I ask about her duties here at the castle since she's already told me she has no family. She's so sweet, and being around her is sort of like having a mother or a grandmother here, even with mine so far away.

We arrive at an exterior door, and she pushes it open. "Enjoy, dear." She pats my shoulder, and I step outside into the most beautiful garden I've ever seen.

A thin layer of snow dusts the ground giving everything an even more magical look. Dozens of flowers are in bloom in every shade imaginable surrounding the outer border and winding around the pathways. I can't name many of them, but I don't have to know their names to appreciate their beauty and their divine scent.

The sound of trickling water has me following a specific path where I find a large decorative fountain. The basin is huge, and above it several wolves raise their faces to what appears to be a hovering moon, though I can barely see the support keeping it in place. Out of their howling mouths water shoots into a smaller basin which pours over into the larger one.

"It's remarkable, isn't it?"

Canaan's voice has my head whipping around. He's standing behind a hedge that comes almost to his waist. I bite my bottom lip and try to keep my face neutral, but it is stunning to see him in this light—and standing—for the first time.

His fur glistens like gold in the light as he slowly makes his way to me. Just like his spine, his legs are twisted, too, and I can see why it might be uncomfortable to walk. I don't offer any assistance, though. I'm sure that would hurt him. He wants to be seen as strong and capable, and I believe he is when it comes to most things, though getting around isn't necessarily one of them.

He comes to stand next to me, and I smile at him. "It's beautiful. Where did it come from?"

"My great-great grandfather had it commissioned," he explains. "It took years for the artist to get it just right. It always brings a smile to my face." He stares up at the fountain, but I am watching him.

Now might be as good a time as any to ask a question that's been lingering in my mind for a while now. "Do you think it's a coincidence that there are pieces like this—a wolf fountain—and other works of art in the house that feature wolves–and your condition?"

He turns to look at me and shakes his head. "No."

I wait for him to say more, but he doesn't. I'm a bit frustrated, but I don't want to ruin the day.

"Shall we explore the garden?" he asks.

"Yes, let's." I place my hand on his arm, and he shudders slightly under my unexpected touch, but then he calms and offers me his elbow, which I take.

Canaan does know the names of the flowers. He lists them for me as we walk along, telling me stories about how his grandmother used to work in the gardens herself because she enjoyed it so much. "I used to attempt to help her, though I think I was more of a burden than anything else."

I giggle, imagining him covered in dirt and digging up the bulbs she's just planted. "I'm sure she enjoyed the time with you."

"I hope so."

After a while, it's clear he's getting a bit tired. Spying a bench, I say, "Let's sit for a bit and admire the scenery."

He doesn't protest, so we have a seat. His bones pop and snap as he lowers himself down on the concrete bench. I pretend not to notice. An amicable silence settles between us, and I breathe in the fresh air, happy to be here with him.

"Are you happy here, Bexley?" he asks me after a while.

"I am." I answer quickly because I don't have to think about it. "Sometimes, it all seems like a dream."

Contented relief settles over him, and he smiles, looking away from me. "I'm glad you like it here, but if that should ever change, please let me know."

"Does it matter?" I'm being frank now. "You said I had to stay for a few months. Almost half that time has passed now. Will I be going home next month?"

When he looks at me again, I think I see a trace of sadness in his eyes. "Do you want to go?"

"I'm honestly not sure how to answer that," I admit. "I love it here. I've made so many friends, and I like spending time with you. I just miss my mother."

"She's still writing to you?"

"Yes, nearly every day. But it's not the same." A longing to embrace my mother fills my heart, and I have to fight back tears.

Canaan rests his paw on my knee. It's comforting. He's never reached over to touch me before, and my body responds in ways it shouldn't. Still, I don't push him away. "I'm sorry, Bexley."

Plastering a smile on my face, I look up at him. "It's okay. But… the girls were talking about how Ellison is going into town today. Do you think it would be possible for me to go?" I don't mention the unrest, leaving it that I only want to see my mother.

He shakes his head. "He left already. Besides, I'm not sure it's safe for you there right now."

"I'm sorry, I don't understand. The girls were saying there's some unrest, partially due to me being gone for so long. If I show them I'm fine, maybe that will die down."

He's more assertive with his response. "Absolutely not, Bexley. I can't allow you to go into the villages, not right now."

Indignation washes over me, and for the first time that I can recall, I'm irritated at him. "I don't understand why not. Just for a few hours—"

"No!" Canaan pulls his hand away and stands. "I've already told you, Bexley. You can't go, and that's final."

Another first—a ripple of fear washes through me. I haven't felt this way since the very first time I saw his silhouette in his office. My brain says he looks like a monster. I pull away from him, plastering myself against the bench.

Immediately, Canaan drags his hand across his face. "I'm so sorry, Bexley. I didn't mean to shout at you. Please forgive me." His yellow eyes shimmer, and I can tell he means it.

"It's fine," I whisper. "I was just trying to help."

"And I appreciate it, but let us handle it, all right?"

I nod and am about to invite him to sit back down when he suddenly goes rigid. His eyes start moving slightly from side to side as if he's carrying on a silent conversation with someone. Then, he says, "I have to go."

"Go? Where?"

He turns and hurries away from me, but it's not that difficult to keep up with him since he's tired. I can imagine he can move quickly in bursts, but not at the moment.

"Something's happened," he says, making his way back down the path that leads to the castle.

"How do you know?"

"I… I can't explain that," he admits. "You should probably go to your room."

"Are we in danger?" I follow him past the fountain and along the walkway I used to access the garden.

"No, not at the moment."

I'm not sure what that means, but alarm begins to build inside of me. I follow him through the door and down the hallway, through the darker recesses of the castle to places I've never been before.

At one point, he slows down a little and looks at what appears to be an ordinary wall, though I can feel a chill seeping through the stones. He says nothing and continues down the hall and turns to the left.

The smell of antiseptic hits my lungs before I realize where we are. It's some sort of a hospital. Canaan passes through a double door and holds it for me. I follow him through.

Everything here is in stark contrast to the dark hallways we traversed to get here. Bright white, sparkling clean, and empty of all décor, it's quite clear this is where the sick and injured are cared for.

Canaan hesitates outside of another door. "Are you sure?"

I nod, not knowing what to expect, and then follow him through to a hospital room.

Ellison is sitting on the edge of it, his shirt off, while Justin inspects what looks like a gunshot wound. I gasp and cover my mouth.

"It's fine!" the patient roars. "I'm fine. Just stop fucking poking me, Justin!"

A woman I don't think I've met before stands next to the physician with a tray of tools. Justin plunks down one bloody instrument and picks up another one. "I will stop poking you as soon as I'm sure I got it all."

"Wh-what happened?" I whisper.

"That bastard fucking shot me," Ellison exclaims, shaking his head.

His hair is sweaty so it doesn't dance around like it normally would. "I should've fucking ripped his head off."

Canaan stays out of the way, and I do, too, but he's nodding like he already knows this. I am so confused. How did he know any of this had taken place?

"You were in my village?" I ask as Justin sets down the last poking device and tells the nurse he's going to close. He washes the wound with something that smells like antiseptic first.

"Yes. It was that bastard Garth."

I take a deep breath, not at all surprised. Tears fill my eyes. "I'm so sorry."

"He says it was a fucking accident, but I don't think so." Ellison narrows his eyes. "The local authorities are investigating." He turns to the king. "You should fucking throw his ass in jail."

"You're probably right," Canaan admits. "But how would that look? Villagers are protesting an absent king. A small caliber firearm accidentally goes off in a crowd wounding one of the king's men, and he arrests the person who claims it was an accident? Wouldn't that make the situation even worse?"

"I don't know," Ellison admits. Justin is struggling to keep him still while he sews him up, not because it hurts but because Ellison is so worked up. "You're probably right. But that man is unhinged."

"You're unhinged," Justin tells him. "Ellison, sit still."

"Here, let me help." I'm not sure what inspires me to step forward when there's a perfectly capable nurse standing right there, but I move to hold Ellison still, placing one hand on his chest and the other on his back, giving him a reassuring smile. My eyes are on Ellison's when he blinks a few times, and his head tips to the side.

"What the hell?" Justin asks, standing still with the needle in place.

It's then that I notice a slight yellow glow emanating from my hands. My eyes widen in horror as I pull them back, holding them up for a moment before tucking them behind my back. This isn't the first time they've felt this way, but this is the brightest I've ever seen them glow.

Horrified, I back up until I hit the wall. Everyone in the room is staring at me with wide eyes. I don't know what to say, and I don't know what to do. The door is on the other side of the room. I'm trapped—and there's something very, very wrong with me.

WITH YOUR HANDS

BEXLEY'S DARK EYES ARE WIDE WITH TERROR AS SHE STANDS PRESSED against the wall in the infirmary. For the first time in ages, I don't feel like I'm the only one in the room who doesn't want anyone to look at them.

I speak first, knowing exactly how she feels. "It's okay, Bexley."

She shakes her head, that mortified look on her face not fading.

"It really is." Justin sets the needle and thread he was trying to use to sew Ellison's wound aside, no longer needing it, and takes a few steps closer to her. She tries to back away, but she can't. "Bexley, you healed his wound. With your hands."

Once more, she shakes her head furiously. "No. That's not possible. I don't know what happened. It must've been… the orange juice I drank for breakfast. It must've… spilled on my hands."

"Damn, I need to get myself some more of that orange juice," Ellison jokes, trying to lighten the mood. It doesn't work. He picks up his shirt, which is bloodied and has a small hole in it, and stands. "Thanks, Bex."

She nods, but her expression doesn't change.

I tell them what they already know. *"Leave us."*

Everyone makes their way out of the room except for Bexley and me. I hate that the light in here is so bright, and all of her attention is on me. At the moment, it's impossible for me to hide. But then, she's the one who is cowering right now.

I pat the table and step away. Like a zombie, she moves from crushing herself against the wall to the place where Ellison was just sitting, only facing me instead of the door, and folds her hands in her lap, her eyes fixed on them. They are normal now.

"Do you believe in magic?" I ask her.

Immediately, she shakes her head. "My family always said it wasn't real. There were rumors of witches and the like in Hexeton, but I never saw anything to make me think it could really exist."

"Haven't you seen magic before, though, Bexley?" I hazard a step closer to her, ignoring the pain in my legs from having stood for so long.

She lifts her face to look at me, and I see her mind crawling through her memories, trying to find the moments I'm referring to.

"The letter that arrived in your mailbox—that was magic."

She shakes her head.

"The way I knew what had happened to Ellison without anyone telling me, without anyone sending word that he was back in the castle. How do you think that happened?"

Again, her head shifts from left to right.

"This." I gesture at my own body, being careful not to reveal too much without leaving her in the dark. "What do you think this is?"

"It—it's a disease," she mutters.

A chuckle escapes my lips, and I shake my head. "You've heard the women talk about fated mates and the Moon Goddess, yes?"

This time, she nods in response.

"Magic. All of it. Our kind—we are magical creatures. I can't tell you everything—also because of magic—but I can assure you that what you have is a magical ability, one I suspected you might have, but I didn't know for sure until just now."

"But—but magic is bad," she blurts as tears spring to her eyes. "Mother says to stay away from magic, that it can only hurt us."

I'm not sure what happened to her father, but I suspect it involved the bad magic she's referring to. I can see why her mother would tell her such a thing. I reach out and lay my paw on her arm. "There is definitely some bad magic in the world. There are evil witches and sorceresses who cast devious spells." I slide my paw down to her hand. "But what you have? That's good magic, Bexley. It's the kind of magic that can help people. Ellison's wound wasn't serious, thank goodness. I suspect Garth was trying to make a point. It's possible it will be worse in the future. We'll have to do what we can to avoid that. But the fact that you were able to heal his wound just by touching him? That's good magic. The best kind of magic."

With tears sliding down her cheeks, Bexley buries her head in my chest. I wrap my arms around her and hold her close. I long to smooth her hair away from her face, to press my lips to hers and assure her that it's all going to be fine, but I can't. The best I can do is hold her awkwardly in my twisted arms and hope to provide some sort of comfort as she questions everything about the world she's ever known.

After a few minutes, she stirs, and I know to release her. "Thank you." She swipes the tears on her cheeks.

"You're welcome." I smile down at her the best I can in this horrid state of mine. "It will be all right, Bexley."

"I hope so." She leans up and presses her lips to my cheek. I close my eyes and revel in the fear of her mouth on me, even if it's hard to feel through my fur.

She slips away from me and darts through the door. I hear Justin ask her if she needs help finding her way back to her room, and she says she can find it. I know she can't, so I send Anna to intercept her, using the mind-link and then walk out into the hallway.

"I guess that answers our question," Justin says, joining me as I head toward my room. "I'm sorry I couldn't get a definitive answer through the tests I've been running. Not a lot of witches willingly give blood samples for comparison."

"Doesn't matter now," I assure him as I begin to walk back to my office. I'm exhausted, but I have to keep going. "We need to figure out what this Garth is up to."

"Ellison said he was babbling on about how you're a monster and the castle is surrounded by wolves. He is claiming you stole his fiancée."

I grimace at the words. Just the thought of Bexley with that bastard makes me want to find him and squeeze his head between my paws until it bursts. "Do we think he's been creeping around the castle?"

"I don't know," Justin admits. "The guards have had to be cautious because Bexley's been outside so much. You didn't want her to see them in their wolf forms."

"Right." I'd been trying not to scare her or clue her in that we are not ordinary people. "Let's increase them, especially if what Ellison says he was shouting about storming the castle is accurate." I can't imagine Garth being able to gather enough citizens to lead a charge on the castle, which is over an hour away by carriage from his village, but the man is obviously mentally unbalanced.

"If they do come, they'll be armed," Justin reminds me as we turn the last corner. My room comes into view ahead, even in the dim light.

He's right. Humans have no qualms about carrying weapons, whereas it is against our kind's honor to fight with anything but teeth and claws.

Our numbers have been low since the spell was cast. It affected everyone who was inside of the castle at the time, making it so they couldn't leave for more than a few hours without becoming extremely ill. The soldiers who were in the barracks or elsewhere were not affected, so many of them chose to go back to their home-lands in the villages on the east side of the mountain. I couldn't compel them to stay, not without showing them what I had become. They heard that my parents were dead, that I was the new king, and that I was in mourning. After the mourning period ended, and I still didn't reveal myself, many of them went home, and I couldn't blame them.

"Let's do our best to reinforce the castle," I say. "Perhaps… Bexley should go address them."

"You think?" Justin stops in his tracks. "But if she leaves the castle before your birthday, before the spell is broken, you might die."

I take a deep breath. "I think the witch said I'd become ill, but I don't know about dying. She may need to go assure them that she's all right and ask them to lay down their arms." The situation in the villages seems to be worse than what I've gathered. At this point, I wouldn't even mind giving them their independence, but I have no idea who to install as the leader, and if I simply remove myself from the situation, they will plummet into chaos and end up with someone like Garth as their self-proclaimed king.

"I think we should hold off on that," Justin warns. "Give it a day or two, and let's see if they calm down. We can send our people in on shifts to monitor the situation."

I find myself nodding along, but something about this situation isn't sitting right with me. "Where's Ellison?"

"I told him to go to his room to rest," he says. "Not that he ever listens. He says he feels fine. Her powers seem to have healed him clean through. It's remarkable."

I'm only half-listening, but I catch the gist. "Yes, it is remarkable, I agree. Where's Bexley? Did Anna escort her to her room?"

"I believe so," he says. "Should we tell her to stay in her room for the time being?"

I want to think that Bexley and everyone else is safe beyond the castle walls, but it's hard to say for sure. "It's probably for the best."

Justin nods. "I'll go tell her."

"Thank you." I walk into my room and collapse on the couch, overwhelmed by all that's transpired. It seems everything is beginning to ramp up. If only the villagers could wait another few weeks. Maybe then, Bexley will have broken the curse, and I'll be able to stand in front of them, a whole man, and assure them that I will do my best to make their lives as prosperous as possible.

But with that madman Garth out there, who knows what might happen. He's wholly unpredictable and dangerous.

And he might just be after Bexley.

I'm not sure how long I've been sitting on the couch mulling everything over when Justin's voice sounds in my head. *"She's not in her room. I'm going to look outside."*

My heart lurches in my chest, and I know something is wrong.

Something is very wrong.

LUNA HOLLOW

Bexley

THE FRESH AIR COOLS MY CHEEKS AND HELPS CLEAR MY MIND AS I crunch through the freshly fallen snow out in the forest. It seems thicker out here, unlike the garden where it was a light dusting. I'm not trying to be quiet so that I can sneak up on any animals at the moment, so I let my footsteps crack, sending an echo through the forest.

I find one of my favorite spots, an area where I've been watching a family of foxes until recently. They were living in a log, but I haven't seen them in a few days. I've seen more large prints out here recently, and I think something must've scared them off.

I've been suspicious that the larger pawprints are from a wolf—or several, honestly. I see a lot of those tracks out here, but I've never seen a wolf. With everything that's happened recently funneling through my mind, I think it's a little strange that I haven't seen a wolf. I think of the fountain, some of the paintings I've seen in the castle, some of the details, and most importantly, Canaan's appearance.

There should be a wolf presence here. Hell, the name of the kingdom is Luna Hollow.

I think about what Canaan said about werewolves that day before he showed himself to me for the first time. Today, he talked to me about magic and about his deformities, implying that he doesn't have a disease at all but that he's been placed under some sort of spell.

A curse, I suppose.

I walk along, kicking up the powdery substance, thinking about what it all means, especially my role in this. How in the world did I heal Ellison just by touching him? I hold my hands out in front of me and stare at them. I've neglected to bring any mittens since I never put them on anyway. My hands look normal now. Sometimes, I get a tingling sensation in them and think that they're glowing a bit, but I've never seen them like they were earlier today.

When I touched Ellison—and closed up a bullet hole.

"Bexley?"

I look up, swiveling around. I hear someone whispering my name, but I don't see anyone. I spin around again as I hear it another time.

Out of the corner of my eye, I see movement at the top of the wide marble fence that separates the castle grounds from the rest of the kingdom. It's at least eight feet tall here, smooth, and impossible to climb. And yet, I see two arms hanging over the top of it before a head pops up and I am staring at a familiar face.

Terror streaks through me as I take several hurried steps backward. "Garth? What the hell are you doing?" I need to get back to the castle. He shot Ellison earlier. He can't be trusted.

He manages to pull himself up to the top of the wall and swing his legs over. I look back toward the castle through the trees, but it's so far away. I can't outrun him, I know that.

"Thank goodness you're outside," he says, panting a bit as he leaps down onto the ground. With the snowdrifts, he's closer to the height of the fence than I realized, and with his long arms, it makes sense that he could climb over if there are drifts on the other side. "Come on, Becky. Let's go."

I glare at him. "A moment ago, you knew my name. What changed?"

He grins at me. "Come on. It's an unflattering name. Becky is much better. Now that I have your attention, I need to get you the fuck out of here. The king has been lying to you to keep you here. I'm sure he's already ruined you, but we need to get back to the village. We need to tell everyone what he's done so they'll join me in the uprising."

Fear and panic wash over me as I hear his words. I shake my head. "No way. None of that's true. The king hasn't done anything to me. I'm not going anywhere with you."

"Becky!" He pulls on the strap that's wrapped around his chest, and that's when I realize he's carrying a rifle. "Come on! You've got to know they're brainwashing you! You have to come back with me. They're terrible, monstrous people. That man who came to speak to us today told us all sorts of lies about how the king will be making an appearance next month, after his birthday. Some of the citizens were actually starting to believe that. We can't let that happen. He doesn't deserve to rule our lands."

"Is that why you shot Ellison?" I bark, angrier than I am afraid all of a sudden. I understand his angle. He doesn't want Canaan to be king of Menschen. It's quite obvious that Garth wants to be the ruler there—and if he had his way, he'd probably be the ruler of the entire kingdom.

He smirks at me and doesn't bother to try to deny it. "They didn't arrest me. I said it was an accident."

"You are despicable, Garth Roberts. I will not go with you, and I wouldn't marry you if it was the only way I could see my mother again. Now, get the hell out of here before I call for the guards!" I look around in the hopes that some guards will appear, but I can't do that magic trick Canaan was telling me about earlier where he suddenly knows things without being told.

I hope somehow he knows about this, too, but I don't want him coming out here, not when Garth is carrying a gun.

I haven't seen a single weapon on anyone in the castle--ever. Not even the guards.

In the distance, I hear howling. Garth looks up and reaches for his rifle, but he doesn't pull it around, not yet. "Becky, they haven't been honest with you. Your mother is very sick. In fact, she's dying." He takes a few steps toward me, a pained expression on his face.

My eyes widen as I imagine my poor mother at home, sick in her bed, possibly dying, and me so far away.

But then, I remember she's been writing me letters almost every day. Not only has she not mentioned being ill, her handwriting is the same as it has always been, and she's been talking about all the cooking she's been doing. "You're lying."

"No, I'm not. You've been getting letters, right?" He steps closer again. I back into a wide tree trunk. I'm trapped. "Well, those are fake. You know how the letters from the king just magically appeared? They're using some sort of evil witchcraft to do that, and they're doing the same thing to manufacture those letters to you. Becky, this whole land is cursed. Don't you know that? The last king and queen were killed by a witch for all the evil they did when they invaded our lands and took them by force. You don't know how bad the war was because you didn't live here."

I shake my head. "Fiona said it was a fairly peaceful takeover. Only a bit of resistance from some of the villages on the outskirts of the territory had casualties."

He scoffs. "That's what they want you to believe. My father fought —and died in that war. Come on, Becky. We don't have time for this. You're coming with me."

Garth lunges at me, and I try to dodge him, but before he reaches me, a blur of golden fur comes flying out from between the trees, knocking him to the ground. I duck behind the tree, covering my mouth to keep from screaming as Canaan tackles Garth to the ground.

The two of them roll around a bit. With Canaan's twisted frame, it's difficult for him to use the razor sharp claws on his hand, but he manages to swipe Garth in the face. He shouts and kicks Canaan off.

The king goes flying across the forest, crashing into a tree. Garth gets to his feet and brings his rifle around.

"No!" I scream, jumping at Garth. The crack of the rifle splinters my hearing as I give him a hard shove. He doesn't fall, though. I spin around, hoping he's missed his mark, but Canaan is sitting on the ground, his hands covering his abdomen. His white shirt is stained red as he raises his yellow eyes at me.

I know what he's thinking. He's going to get up and come at Garth again—and I can't let him do that.

Throwing myself between them, I place both hands on Garth's shoulders. "No! Please, I'm begging you, don't."

"What the fuck is that?" Garth shouts, looking over my shoulder. "That's not a fucking wolf. It's a goddamn monster!"

I rear back and slap him hard in the face. I want to do more, like raise my knee and ram it into his groin, but Garth has me by the wrist, twisting. "You fucking bitch!" I bite back a scream so that Canaan doesn't know he's hurting me.

Behind me, he growls, "Bexley, move."

"No." I turn my head and look at him. Tears fill my eyes as I meet his gaze. "No. I can't do that."

He narrows his gaze at me, and I hear howling growing closer.

That's when everything snaps into place.

The guards are wolves. The people are wolves. The wolves are people.

I turn back to Garth. "Let's go."

"What?" He's looking around now for the wolves. "Where are they?"

"They're coming, and you can't shoot them all," I remind him. But he could shoot some of them, and that won't work for me—not if I can save them. "I will go with you if you let me tell Canaan goodbye."

"Canaan?" Garth's forehead puckers. "That fucking monster is the goddamn king?"

"Will you give me a second to say goodbye, and then I will go with you?" I bark, watching him freak out.

"Yes, yes," he finally manages. "But if you try anything, I'll shoot him in the fucking head."

Somehow, Canaan has gotten to his feet. He's bleeding badly. He comes toward Garth, but I block him. "It's okay," I tell him, looking into his eyes. "It's going to be okay."

"You cannot go with him, Bexley," he says through gritted teeth.

"I have to. Otherwise, he'll kill you. He's not fighting fair, Canaan."

From over by the wall, I hear Garth shouting, "Becky, come on!"

I place my hand on Canaan's wound and see a yellow glow. It's not enough. This wound is far worse than Ellison's was, and I can't stand here long to heal it fully, but I know he will live. I lift up on my tiptoes and press my lips to his, not caring that he has razor sharp fangs and a crooked mouth.

I want to tell him everything I'm feeling in my heart, but I can't. Not with Garth at the top of the wall extending an arm to me. I see wolves tearing in from all directions now. I meet Canaan's eyes for a moment and then rush toward Garth. I grab his hand, and he pulls me over the wall just as a large wolf with green eyes comes into view. I know that it's Ellison. I lift my hand, and then we are gone.

TAKEN BY A MADMAN

CANAAN

PAIN RIPPLES THROUGH MY ABDOMEN DESPITE BEXLEY'S POWERS blanketing me in the soft light of her healing powers. It's not just the gunshot wound that hurts. As I see her disappear over the wall in Garth's grasp, I feel my insides begin to shatter.

"We'll get her back!" Ellison shouts in my head. He's a huge wolf and can jump over that wall, I know it, but he'll only have a couple of hours to track them down once he's there. We need a plan.

"You six, go with Ellison," I command, keeping a hand pressed against my stomach as I point with the other at the men I mean to go with him. I can hear horse hooves in the distance and know that Garth has a head start. My men will be faster, but the snow is beginning to fall, and that will make it more difficult to stay on his tracks and will help cover the scent.

Something tells me Garth has more tricks up his sleeve.

Justin is at my side in his human form dressed only in a pair of pants he likely grabbed from one of the stashes the guards keep in the woods in case they have to shift. "Let me see," he demands.

Reluctantly, I move my hand aside. Around me, chaos ensues as Ellison backs up and takes a running leap at the fence. He makes it over, but it sounds like a hard landing on the other side. "Are you all right?" I call out.

"Fine," he grumbles in my head. *"Come on!"* I wish he was speaking to me, but he's not. In my present state, I cannot make that leap.

"The bleeding has stopped here." Justin walks around and looks at the exit wound, which is clearly visible through the hole in the back of my shirt. "Here, too. Does it still hurt?"

"No." It's the truth, my gut doesn't hurt anymore, and neither does the smaller wound in my back. But already, with Bexley only a mile or so away, my heart is beginning to ache, and it's getting harder to breathe. I have to work through it. "We have to defend the castle," I remind Justin. "There's a chance he'll use what he saw here to rally the villagers. Bexley said my name. He knows I'm a monster.'

Justin stands before me, his hands raised, a calm expression in his eyes. "All right. We'll do that. But I think you need to go lie down."

"What? Why the fuck would I do that when—" I can't get the words out before I tumble backward. Justin grabs me before I hit the ground, and a couple of the other guards rush in as well. He's shouting orders like he's the king, and I guess he may as well be now, with me out of commission and Ellison gone. My heart is being crushed in a vice, and I can't pull in a complete breath.

"Get him back to his room," Justin shouts. The guards lift me off the ground and awkwardly carry my twisted body toward the castle. It's slow-going because I'm heavy, it's snowing, and we're in the thickest part of the forest a good distance away from the castle. Why couldn't Bexley just spend her time in the back garden?

I attempt to use the mind-link to give some more orders, but my thoughts are jumbled. The further away from me Bexley gets, the more the world begins to fade.

We are almost to the castle when I can no longer open my eyes. The pain in my chest is excruciating. I finally surrender, and everything goes black.

Bexley

Pressed against Garth's chest, I hold onto the saddle horn as the horse speeds through the falling snow. Garth is pushing it as hard as he can, winding through the forest, taking trails that I can barely see.

"What the actual fuck is that thing?" he asks, the shocked tone from earlier lingering in his voice. "I've never seen anything so hideous in my life."

"That thing is your king," I remind him, shouting to be heard since I can't easily turn my head and don't want to look at him anyway. It's bad enough that we're sitting so close together. In the distance, I hear howls and know that means Canaan has sent some of his guards after us. I wish he hadn't. I don't want anyone else getting shot if I can prevent it. I'll see my mother and then find a way to get back to the castle once I make Garth see reason. He's power hungry at the moment, but hopefully I can convince him that the king is good and kind.

"He might be our king for now, but he won't be for long," he chuckles, and some of the hysteria from earlier seems to fade as he thinks about his nefarious plans.

"What do you mean?" I ask, afraid to hear the answer.

"You're all the proof I needed," he explains, directing the horse beneath a tree. We both have to duck to miss a low hanging branch. "As soon as we get to the others and they see that that monster has assaulted you, well, they'll be ready to attack."

"But the king hasn't attacked me," I tell him. "They won't believe it when there is no proof."

A low rumble sounds in his throat as up ahead of us a barn looms. "Oh, Becky. You're so naïve," he says. "When I show them the proof of the torture you've been through at the hands of the king, you won't be able to argue with me."

"What do you mean?" I ask, but all I get in response is an evil laugh.

And then, it all falls into place.

He's going to take me into that barn, force himself upon me, beat me senseless, and tell everyone in the village that Canaan did it so they will storm the castle, kill the king and all the occupants, and then install him as king.

My stomach tightens at the thought of it. He's lied about everything—including my poor mother who is just fine at home right now but won't be once she finds out what's happened to me. And she'll have no way of knowing it was Garth.

No one will know.

"No!" I shout, struggling against him. I push his arm, but it barely moves, only making him laugh again. The wolves howl again, but somehow they seem further away. I can't wait for their help. I have to act now.

With no other choice, I grab hold of Garth's arm and sink my teeth down into the soft area right above his wrist, ignoring the metallic taste that fills my mouth as he screams and I fight to rip a chunk out.

"You fucking bitch!" He wrenches his arm around me and brings it up to hit me hard in the side of the head. I throw my elbow back into his ribs and ignore the pain as the horse gets spooked and rears up on its hindlegs.

Using this angle to my advantage, I push backward, digging my feet into the horse's ribcage and twist my body as I continue to jab. Garth fights back, trying to hit me as he wars against the horse. He connects with my jaw, and a sharp pain slices through my head, but I can't pay attention to that. I bring the heel of my hand down into his groin, and he screams again.

The horse rears up once more, and this time, we both go tumbling off the back. I land hard on top of Garth who temporarily has the wind knocked out of him. I kick him in the balls and stomp on his stomach before I turn to run.

I only get a few steps before he grabs my ankle, and I hit the ground hard, barely breaking my fall with my hands. "You stupid whore!" he says as he drags me toward him. "I should fucking kill you right here."

"Let me go!" I twist around and try to kick him in the face with my other leg, but he grabs that one, too. Blood pours from his arm, coating the snow in scarlet.

"I guess I'll just have to go ahead and do this right here." He pulls my legs apart as he slides up my body, pinning one leg with his thigh as he reaches for his zipper.

The howls are still too far away.

He's got his pants down, and he's reaching for my skirt.

"No!" I shout, the world starting to blur around me.

Garth laughs.

I lift my hands, thinking I must try to push him off again, but as I bring them around, I realize they are glowing.

Not yellow—but purple.

"No!" I scream again, and this time a bolt of light flies from both of my palms, hitting Garth squarely in the chest. He goes shooting off me, the scent of singed hair filling the air as he slams down on the ground near a large rock.

I take a deep breath and stagger to my feet, the world still spinning. I have no idea how that happened, but I can't dwell on it now. I have to get away.

I have to get back to the castle to warn the others that Garth is trying to start a war.

Scrambling to my feet, I fix my dress and look around. Gunfire sounds in the distance. I freeze for a moment. Did the villagers intercept the wolves that were coming to my rescue? "No," I whisper, shaking my head. This can't be happening.

Behind me, Garth grunts. I should take his gun. I should shoot him with it. But I can't take the risk of him getting me in his clutches again. I see his spooked horse standing about a hundred yards from me and slowly approach it.

This will not be easy, but I haven't spent my entire life studying animals for one of them to fail me now. "Come here, sweetie," I say in my calmest voice. "It's okay." I lift up my hands and slowly approach.

The horse whinnies and backs a few steps away, then tosses his head as if to tell me he doesn't like this.

"I know. I know." I get a bit closer, and he calms a bit snorting. He's well-trained, even if he wasn't particularly happy with his owner.

Gently, I reach out and place my palm on his nose. He whinnies, and I grab the reins. I hear Garth groaning again and know I'm out of time.

"That's a good boy," I coo. "Come on, baby." I get a foot in the stirrups and throw my leg over the saddle. This horse is massive; it has to be to carry Garth around, so once I'm seated, I can't reach the stirrups. I lower myself down near the saddle horn and say, "Let's go," coaxing him back the way he came. I'm a decent rider from all the time I spent at my grandparents' place, so I trust I can keep myself in the saddle as we rush back the way we came.

I pray I get there in time to warn Canaan.

STORM THE CASTLE!

CANAAN

THE WORLD AROUND ME IS MUFFLED AS I TRY TO OPEN MY EYES. THE intense pain I felt right before I passed out is still present, though I can't feel it quite as sharply now as I could before. Justin hovers over me, holding a bottle under my snout. I assume it's some sort of smelling salts. I almost wish he hadn't bothered. I think I'd rather be out when my entire body feels like I've been trampled by a thousand stampeding horses.

"Ellison and the others are under attack," he says, jarring me back to reality. I try to sit up, but he won't let me. "A mob of armed citizens intercepted them a few miles on the other side of the castle grounds. Three of the six guards you sent are down, and he's wounded again. I told him to get back here, but he won't listen. We need another plan. They lost track of Bexley, and they're just getting slaughtered."

I nod in acknowledgement. He's not wrong. With a deep breath, I close my eyes to concentrate and call out to my other best friend through the mind-link. *"Ell, get back here, now. That's an order."*

"I can't do that, Alpha." I can hear the pain in his voice, even though

he's miles away, and our connection isn't that strong. *"I have to find her."*

"No one wants to find her more than I do," I assure him. *"But this isn't working. I need you to get back here safely and defend the castle."*

He's silent for a long moment, which makes me wonder if he's okay. Surprisingly, I am beginning to feel a bit better and find myself able to sit up as I wait for a response.

Finally, Ellison asks, *"Is the castle under attack?"*

"Not presently," I admit, *"but I have no doubt Garth intends to use Bexley and what he saw here as fuel to lead a revolt. I'm sure they'll storm the castle."*

"Fuck," he mutters. *"What are we going to do about her? If we don't get her back to the castle soon, you'll die. Right? Isn't that how it works?"*

"That was my understanding," I admit. *"But I'm all right at the moment. How many warriors do you have left?"*

"Three." His tone is dismal.

I don't bother to ask who has fallen at this point because I don't want him to dwell on it. *"Head home."*

"Yes, Alpha."

With that, I end the mind-link and open my eyes. "They're coming back, but I won't be surprised if a mob doesn't follow."

Justin nods grimly. "We should get the women and children to safety. Should we send them to the vault?"

My stomach tightens for a moment, and it has nothing to do with the intense pain I'm still experiencing. We were so close! So close to all of this being over. Bexley even kissed me before she left. How can we be back in a situation where everything is falling apart?

"Alpha?" Justin repeats.

"Yes," I tell him. "Get them into the vault."

He nods and takes off. I hear Anna protesting in the hallway, saying she doesn't want to leave me, and I'm sure Naomi will also put up a fight, but Olive will convince her to go. The other women should go more readily. Most of them are staff or elderly nobles who rarely leave their rooms.

Still, the vault is the last place that anyone would want to be.

I try to sit up again, and while the pain in my chest doesn't hurt as much as it did before for reasons I can't explain, the shotgun wound is beginning to fester inside. I look down at the hole in my shirt and see that the outside is healed up nicely, but I wonder if there's still something going on inside of my body. My organs are not where they should be thanks to my deformities so it's hard to say what might've been hit, and Justin hasn't cut me open to take a look.

He probably thought I was going to die of a broken heart anyway.

I need to get out of this bed and go help organize our defenses. I have no idea how many armed villagers are about to show up at my doorstep, but I don't think it'll be more than a hundred or so. We should be able to hold them off.

Except they have guns—and we have none.

Justin rushes back into the room. "How are you?"

"Fine," I lie. "Can you help me up?"

"No," he says flatly. "You don't need to get up. In fact, I need to lock you in here."

"No, you don't." I glare at him. "I need to organize the troops."

"I can do that," he insists.

"You're a healer, not a warrior." I prop myself up a little further on my elbow and grimace.

"I'll figure it out. Stay here." He tries to pin me to the bed with a glare and takes off.

I curse and attempt to swing my back paws off the bed, but they're not having it. I curse again, give up, and collapse.

"Alpha, a horse is approaching up the lane to the castle, moving at a fast rate," one of the guards says in my head.

My first thought is that it's Garth back to shoot me again. I tell the guard, *"Get ready for an attack, but assess as needed."*

"Yes, Alpha," he replies, and once again, I push up off the mattress. This time, I make it to sitting before Justin shoots through the door.

"Come to the window," he insists.

I start to stand, almost fall, and feel his hand clamp around my arm. I thank him and try again with his assistance. Carefully, he steers me to the window and throws open the curtains.

Night is beginning to settle over the valley below us which makes what we are looking at even easier to see.

Torches. Hundreds of them. They're still in the distance, maybe twenty miles away, but at the speed they're moving, I have to believe they're moving in on horseback, which means they should be here within an hour. It is a steep climb up the mountain, and we keep the road full of ruts on purpose. Still, we are about to have more visitors than I anticipated.

At least two dozen more torches are much closer to the castle. I can see them on the road near the gate, the same one that is closing at the moment. "Is Ellison back?" I ask.

"No, not yet. I believe they had to take a different route. Those are the people that were shooting at them coming up the mountain now."

I take a deep breath and try to use my brain, but nothing is coming to me. "Maybe I should try going out to speak to them."

"They'll shoot you again, Canaan," he says.

"I don't know what else to do."

"We fight," he says. "We shift and fight and defend our home."

I look at him and nod, but the problem is, I can't do any of those things. I can't shift. I can't fight. And I can't defend my home. I feel completely hopeless.

As if reading my mind, he says, "You fought against Garth earlier. If he'd fought fairly, you would've beaten him."

I shake my head. "None of these bastards are going to fight fairly. I can't even stand up at the moment, Justin. I'm leaning on you!"

"We'll defend our home," he promises me.

I nod and release him, leaning against the window.

"*Alpha, we're back,*" Ellison says in my head. "*I found a set of horse hoof prints along the outer wall that don't match the set Garth left earlier.*"

Alarmed, I straighten up. "*Where at?*"

"*We came up from further south than where we crossed to try to lose the mob, which is apparently approaching the front gate,*" he tells me. "*I jumped the fence and found a trail of blood leading toward the castle. It's faint, and the snow is covering it. I'm tracking it now. The footprints are hard to read with all this snow, but I think Garth might be back.*"

"What the fuck?" I ask as I hear a commotion downstairs in the foyer. I turn toward the door as Justin shoots away to see what the trouble is.

Seems like at least one invader has infiltrated the castle—my home—and I need to defend it.

WORTH FIGHTING FOR

Bexley

I rush toward the castle, urging the horse to go as fast as possible, snow falling furiously around us. I have to warn Canaan. Not only is there a mob of villagers approaching the castle, Garth is somewhere behind me. He must've taken a horse from that barn.

The guards at the gate listened to my shouts to let me in, so I didn't even have to slow down as I rode through the front gate. I practically leap off the horse and rush inside as a commotion in the front foyer greets me. "Where's the king?" I shout as David throws open the door.

"Miss Bexley, you're back," he says, locking the door behind me and slipping a heavy bar into place. It's a good thought, but I don't think it will stop the attack that's about to happen. They'll figure out a way to get through the gates and then the doors, whether it's this one or one of several others. The castle was built as a luxury home for the royal family, not as a fortress. Clearly, the Zephyrs felt invincible when they constructed this palace.

"The king is upstairs," another servant I've only met a few times tells me. "All of the women have been moved to safety, miss. You should go there as well."

"No," I say, pushing past him and the others on my way to the stairs. Justin is coming down. "We're under attack," I tell him.

"Yes, we know. I'll show you to the vault. Naomi and Olive are there." He reaches for my arm, but I pull it back.

"I need to see Canaan first," I tell him.

"Bexley, there's no time for that," he begins, but I rush past him. He could grab me if he wanted to, but he doesn't. I make it up the stairs and rush toward the back of the castle to Canaan's room, praying he's all right. I don't know how helpful my blast of magic was.

I'm almost to his room when he steps out into the hallway. Relief washes over me, and I rush toward him, careful not to push him backward as I wrap my arms around him.

"Bexley, you're safe." He runs his hand over my hair. "Thank the Goddess."

"They're coming," I tell him. "We've got to hide… or something."

"Yes, you need to get to the vault. It's the safest place in the castle. I'll ask a servant to show you how to get there." He manages a smile, but I can see the hopeless look in his eyes.

I'm not sure what he's planning to do, but it can't be good.

"Canaan, you should come, too. Garth was right behind me. He's probably here already. He wants to kill you and take the throne."

"We'll stop him," he assures me. "We'll protect our home."

"He's already shot you once," I remind him. "You're injured. You can't possibly fight against him. Come with me."

I hear footsteps approaching and turn, lifting my hands and praying that purple light is back if I need it, but it's just Justin, so I lower them, but not before he and Canaan see the new power I've apparently acquired.

"What the hell is that?" Justin asks.

"It's… uhm… some kind of zapping power," I stutter. "I used it to knock Garth out."

"What?" Canaan asks, scooping his hand underneath my wrist and lifting it up to take a look. "You can shoot powers out of your hands that hurt people?"

"Well, when you put it like that...."

"Cool!" Justin says with a smile. "That'll come in handy."

"Absolutely not," Canaan interjects. "She is going to the vault."

"But Alpha, we may need her help," Justin argues.

"He's right. Let me help," I argue. "If you're not going to hide, then why should I?"

He shakes his head, but then both of them freeze, and I know they've got some sort of message going on in their heads again. They always make that face when they're reading each other's minds.

"What is it?" I ask, tugging on his sleeve.

Canaan looks at Justin and then at me. "Ellison found a broken door," he says. "Someone is already in the castle."

"It's Garth," I say. "It has to be."

The king lets out a deep breath and turns to me. Justin steps away to give us some privacy. "Bexley, listen to me. I need you to go with Justin and hide in the vault, okay? I know you don't want to, but I won't be able to concentrate if I don't know for certain you're safe."

"Safe for now," I reply. "But what about when he kills you and everyone else in the castle? What then? We women just slink out and surrender? No. Let me fight. I can do it." I will my hands to glow that purple light, and I must be getting better at it because I can do it on demand this time.

He opens his mouth to say something when distinct gunfire rings out below us.

"I need to go," Justin says.

Canaan nods, and Justin rushes off. Before he turns the corner, he leaps into the air, and before my very eyes, he is suddenly not a human anymore. His clothes shred and fall away, and a magnificent gray wolf rushes down the hallway out of sight.

"Oh, my god!" I murmur, covering my mouth with my hand. "You guys really are wolves."

"Well, they are." Canaan's expression is solemn as he watches.

"That's what happened, isn't it?" I ask. "You're stuck—mid-shift. Right?"

Shaking his head, he says, "I can't talk about that right now, okay? You have to go. Please, Bexley. Go that way toward the darkest part of the castle. When you're almost to the infirmary, there's a stone in the wall that is slightly rounded at the top and a bit more gray than the others. When you find it, push it in, and the vault will open. Go inside and hide with the other women, okay?"

My whole body is shaking as I try to tell him no, but there's more shooting, howling and screaming. It has to be more than just Garth that has made it inside now. I feel a tear slip down my cheek.

Every second I spend arguing with him is wasted. He's in charge of those people down there, the ones Garth is shooting dead, and he needs to be there. Fear paralyzes me as I look into his eyes. There's so much I want to say to him, but it all gets tangled inside, and I can't get any of it.

"Go, my love," he says, giving me a shove. I hear footsteps coming down the hall now, heavy and resounding, so I turn the other way, the direction he's told me to go, and I take off running. I don't know if it's the right idea, but I can't think straight. I turn the corner just before I hear a roar and the floor shakes beneath my feet.

I run until I can't hear it anymore, the sounds of battle, the potential sound of Canaan dying. I run through the darkness, trying to remember how we got to the hospital. I run with tears streaking my face. I run with an image of Canaan in my mind. He oscillates between his twisted wolf form and that glimpse of him I got from the portrait in the library, the version of him I see in my dreams.

I take a wrong turn, spin around and run back the other way. I hear howling from downstairs, multiple gunshots, someone shouting to torch the castle. That will be difficult to do with so much marble, but where there's a will, there's a way.

Tearing down another hallway, I realize I'm lost again. Confused and bawling now, I sink to the floor, wrapping my arms around my knees.

None of this is fair! Canaan doesn't deserve to be trapped in a deformed body. He's the kindest, most intelligent man I've ever met. He would be the best king if only he had the opportunity to show the people who he really is, but he can't do that because of his deformities. He would terrify everyone. I know that. I understand why he hides. Which means, he's become inconsequential to the villagers. They think they want him out. They believe Garth's lies that he's a monster and that he's holding me against my will. They have to see the truth.

I can't prove to them that he's not a monster right now, but I can show them that I'm alive and well.

More than that, I need to do what I can to protect the man I love.

"The man I… love," I repeat.

Does he love me, too? I think back to the last thing he said to me. He'd called me, "my love." That could be just a term of endearment, but I don't think so.

I think he does love me, too.

And I'm willing to fight for that.

With my hands glowing purple, I stand and trace my steps back the way I came.

Back to Canaan.

FIGHT TO THE DEATH

Canaan

The moment Bexley disappears behind me, I turn and rush down the hallway as quickly as I can. When I turn the corner, I see one of my warriors lying in a pool of his own blood with Garth stalking toward him, his rifle still smoking.

A roar tears through my body. Even though I can't shift, that won't stop me from launching myself at the bastard. He doesn't get his weapon up in time, so when I crash into him, I crush it against his body and rip into his shoulders with my gnarled teeth.

"Get off me, you fucking bastard!" Garth shouts, attempting to kick me off like he did last time. I dig my claws in and continue to maul him the best I can. I don't know what's happening downstairs, but this asshole needs to die. Blood and muscle fills my mouth as I chew through him, spitting it aside.

He shouts in anger and pain and tries again to push me off. This time, he uses his elbow for leverage and manages to roll me over. He lifts the butt of the rifle and rams it into my face before I can block him. Pain rockets through my right eye, and I'm pretty sure he snapped my orbital bone, but the pain is nothing compared to how I felt when he took Bexley from me.

Bexley. I'm fighting for her. He raises the weapon to slam it into me again, and I use his shift in weight to my advantage, leaning in the opposite direction and thrusting up with my hind legs. In this position, they're more powerful than a human's, even a large one like Garth. I rocket him off me, and he slams into the wall, taking out a table and one of my mother's favorite vases. It shatters all over the floor.

Scrambling to my feet isn't an option at this point. I'm weak and wounded, with blood pouring down one side of my face. I hear more gunshots, screams, and howls from downstairs. A particularly loud crash has Garth turning his head for an instant, which allows me to push off the wall and get back to my feet.

He still has his rifle, so I need to do something to keep him from shooting me. He's lying in a pile of broken porcelain, each movement grinding it into his flesh. With him struggling to get up for a moment, I dash into the nearest parlor and pick up a table, knowing he'll follow. My paws, slick with blood, slip on the surface, but I manage to keep it in my grasp.

Garth pokes his head in, pulls out, and then steps in, and I slam the table into his head, ramming him into the opposite wall. He grunts and pushes back, shoving me off balance. I fall backward onto a couch. He lifts his rifle and takes aim.

I can't get out of this situation. If I could shift fully, I might be able to fight him off, to tackle him to the ground and rip his throat out, but his bleeding shoulder is a reminder of how impossible it is for me to sink my teeth into anything fully.

He'll pull the trigger in a moment, and I'll be dead. I pray to the Moon Goddess that Bexley is safely tucked away in the vault and absently wonder if the curse will break when I die or if it will go on forever.

But Garth isn't pulling the trigger. Instead, he's standing there with a rifle pointed at my head, chuckling.

"You really thought you were going to win?"

Oh, so it's going to be one of these types of death. A soliloquy. Doesn't he know how often this ends badly for the person prolonging the situation?

"You haven't won anything," I grind out. "This isn't over yet, Garth."

"It is for you." He's still chuckling. "I'm going to blow whatever brains you have in that deformed head of yours all over the wall, finish killing all of your so-called warriors, and then find Becky. When I do, I'm to drag her by her hair right back here and fuck her senseless right next to your headless body."

An uncontrollable rage boils up inside of me. I roar like a lion, pushing up off the couch and launching myself at him in one fluid motion, just as if I've shifted.

I don't make it across the room, though.

The bullet enters my shoulder near my neck and projects straight down. I can practically feel it lodging somewhere near my hip. Pain shoots through me, the agony almost as intense as I'd felt when Bexley left. I hang in the air for a moment before dropping to the ground.

"Stupid fucking bastard," Garth says as he rams the iron-tipped toe of his boot into my shoulder. All I can do is grunt. He kicks me in the head and then straddles me. I open the one eye I can and see the muzzle of his rifle. "You thought you could kill me?" His laughter warbles around me as blackness fills my field of vision. "I guess I was wrong. I'll have to splatter your brains all over this pretty carpet instead." He cocks the rifle, and I close my eyes.

BEXLEY

I TEAR DOWN THE HALLWAY, LETTING MY PURPLE LIGHT ILLUMINATE MY pathway. I hear a struggle and then a gunshot ring out and know I'm almost back to the place where I said goodbye to Canaan. I round the corner and come to a stop in front of an open door.

Garth stands in the room, a rifle poised over a person I can't see who's prone on the floor. I have to believe it's Canaan, though. He cocks the rifle and takes aim.

"Wait!" I shout.

"Oh, good! You're here, Becky." He turns to face me. "Just in time. You'll save me the time and energy to go track you down. Not that I mind. Hunting is my specialty, after all. I should probably save this bastard's head to hang on the wall in my den, but I think it'll be much more satisfying to blow his brains out."

"You don't have to do that, Garth." Panic thrums through my body as I take a few cautious steps toward him. "I told you last time I'd go with you if you don't kill him."

"Yes, and then you bit the hell out of my arm, crushed my nutsack, and used some kind of fucked up magic to blast me across the forest."

Canaan chuckles, and Garth kicks him, hard, and then steps toward me, giving Canaan the opportunity to roll away. He's still close enough for Garth to do exactly what he said and shoot him in the head, but at least he's got a bit of room now.

I don't know what I expect to happen here. My hands aren't purple at the moment as I hope to coax Garth out. Maybe I can stall long enough for Ellison or Justin to get here.

"Maybe it would be better if I fucked you in front of the bleeding, dying king," Garth continues. "What would you think about that, Princess?"

"I think… I think it would be difficult for you to do that since your dick is the size of a baby carrot." I'm treading on thin ice here, but I've got to give Canaan a chance. Maybe he can hit him over the back of the head or something.

"What the fuck did you say?" He moves close to me and lifts the rifle so that it's pointing at me now. "You stupid bitch. You don't know what the fuck you're talking about."

"Don't I? I saw it in the woods the last time you threatened to rape me, remember?"

"Well, that might've seemed like a threat, but this is a promise." He moves closer to me still. "And if you raise your glowy hands, I will shoot you."

I can't see Canaan at all now, but I think he's probably still lying on the floor somewhere on Garth's right. He's only a few steps away from me now, the rifle ready to blow my head off if I take one more step. One of us is about to die, and I don't think it's going to be Garth.

If it's me or Canaan, or both, I need him to know the truth of the situation. I need him to know what I was too panicked to say earlier. "Garth, you don't understand. It's too bad you've never found your person."

"My… what?"

"Your person. Your true love. Your fated mate, as they call it here in the castle. Maybe someone hurt you when you were a child, or maybe you're just an evil person, I don't know, but I feel sorry for you. When you die, your soul is going to rot in hell for eternity. When I die, well, I'll be surrounded by love."

"Charming, Becky," he says, cocking his head to the side. "We're both going to die one day, but the two of you are going first. I'm going to fuck you, shoot him, and go rule his kingdom."

"No," I tell him, knowing what I have to do. My hands begin to tingle. I can't let him kill Canaan. If he shoots me, so be it, but I will blast the ever living fuck out of him with my powers before I let that happen. "Canaan, if you can hear me, I don't care what you look like. I love you."

Garth chuckles. "Well, isn't that sweet. Now get over here, Becky!"

I lift my hands and hit him with every ounce of power I can muster. "It's Bexley, you bastard!"

Garth goes flying backward, and just as my light starts to fade, an enormous golden wolf leaps from behind the door, latching onto his neck. My eyes widen in shock and wonder at the massive size of Canaan's wolf. He's easily six feet tall with paws the size of my head.

There is no struggle. Garth hits the ground, lets out a squeal of some kind, and then goes still. The distinct smell of urine mixes with the metallic odor of blood hanging in the air as he soils himself.

When Canaan turns to face me, he's holding Garth's severed head in his teeth.

LET'S NOT LOSE OUR HEADS

BEXLEY

I WANT TO RUN TO CANAAN AND WRAP MY ARMS AROUND HIS FURRY neck, but we can't do that right now. The sounds of fighting from downstairs are still intense, and it's clear he's still injured. He drops Garth's head on the floor, and I rush over to him, trying to see where the bullet entered him earlier.

He nuzzles up against me, and I almost laugh, but I'm too busy looking for his injury. I find it in his shoulder. "This looks painful," I murmur, wishing he could talk to me. His eye is also a bit jacked up, like maybe Garth also punched him too hard in the face.

"I'm all right," I hear in my head.

I take a step backward and almost trip over what's left of Garth. "Wh-what was that?"

He looks at me with a wolfy grin. *"That's the mind-link. I can talk to you now that you know who you are."*

"Now that I know who I am?" I repeat, having no idea what he's talking about. I shake my head and put my hands on his wounded shoulder and over his eye. Instantly, that calming, warm, yellow glow takes over, and his smile widens. "You're going to have to explain all of this to me later, once we take the castle back."

"I will, I promise," he says. *"But maybe you should stay behind. I don't want you to get hurt."*

I narrow my eyes at him. "How did that work out for you last time, Your Majesty?"

"Fair point. But I'm in much better shape to fight now than I was before."

"Still, I'm coming with you. I want everyone to know that Garth is dead, and the coup is over." I place my hands on my hips to let him know I mean what I'm saying.

Canaan nods and then stares at Garth's decapitated head. *"Maybe you should bring that. Just for emphasis."*

I wrinkle my nose. The bleeding from the severed head isn't much compared to the body, but I really don't want to touch it. "No, thank you."

He's laughing in my head, and I love the sound of it. Already, he seems like a different person to me—not that he needed to change. But he seems freer and happier than he was before he was able to shift into this magnificent wolf.

The chuckling stops as he picks Garth's head up with his teeth again and carries it out the door. I follow behind, hoping that we aren't about to find all of our troops dead. Canaan walks slow enough for me to keep up, but I know he wants to run.

When we reach the stairs, the signs of carnage are already evident. Dead bodies of the villagers as well as some slain wolves lay in various positions along the landing and the steps. In the foyer, I see a wolf attempting to drag himself out of harm's way while a villager rushes at him with a gun.

"Stop!" I shout, lifting my hand. I hit the villager with my purple light, and he goes flying backward, hitting a wall. This catches the attention of several of the other men with guns. About five weapons turn toward us. Canaan growls, and I tell them, "Hold your fire, or I will send all of you flying against the wall."

"Hey, it's her!" one of them shouts. "The kidnapped girl!"

"What the fuck is that?" another one asks, looking at Garth's head.

Canaan lets it go, and the severed cranium rolls all the way down the stairs, leaving a trail of crimson in the center of each step. It rolls to a stop at the foot of the stairs.

"That is the man you foolishly followed into battle," I tell them. "Drop your weapons now, or else you'll suffer the same fate."

"But… there's fucking werewolves in here!" another man says.

"They're not werewolves," I tell them. How I know this, I'm not sure, but when Canaan supplies a different word in my head, I repeat it. "They're wolf shifters. They're people, just like you and me, but they have the ability to take on the form of wolves."

"So the rumors are true," an older man says. "It was wolves who defeated us in the war and took our lands."

Canaan supplies the narrative in my head so I can explain. "No, that's not what happened. King Paul held a meeting with the town council. They agreed to the territory becoming part of Luna Hollow. It was only a handful of resisters who rose up against King Paul when he was leaving that lost their lives. You all should remember this. It only happened a few years ago."

"But Garth said his father was slaughtered in battle by soldiers who fought alongside wolves," one of them protests.

"Garth is an idiot," I remind them. "I'm here of my own free will."

"Tell them you're going to be their next queen," Canaan says in my head.

I'm repeating everything he says, so I say, "I'm going to be your next queen," before realizing what he's said. Then I stop and turn to him. "Wait—what?"

He's got that wolfish grin back on his face. I raise my eyebrows and shake my head. "We'll talk about this later," I whisper.

The group at the bottom of the stairs has grown as the fighting has stopped and others have come into the room. "Queen? But you're not even human yourself," one of the first men I interacted with says.

"Of course I am. What are you talking about?" I ask him.

"I saw that strange purple light come out of your hands and send William flying against the wall," he reminds me.

I look at all of their stunned faces. "I… don't know how that happened. But I know I also have the power to heal. I'd like to show all of you. I'd like to heal all of the injured and discuss the terms of your surrender. While atonement will need to be made for the lives you've claimed today, your king understands you were led astray by a madman with an agenda. If we can stop this fight right now, if all of you will surrender, we can negotiate fair terms. Otherwise, we will go back to fighting. All of you will die, and I won't have the opportunity to save any of the injured."

"Where is the king?" a man I've seen with Garth a few times in the market says. "If he would've just shown his face once in a while, none of this would have happened."

"This is your king." I gesture at Canaan. "And he will be addressing the entire village soon. He's been ill for quite some time, but now, he's better, and he's going to be a king for all the people."

"Did you heal him with your shiny light?" another townsperson wants to know.

"*Yes*," Canaan supplies.

It's not quite accurate, but it's clear to me we can't tell them all the details. "I healed him," I assure them. "Now, what say you?" I ask like the queen I'm, apparently, about to become. "Are you ready to surrender?"

For a moment, no one moves. I feel my hands start to tingle in case they start shooting again. But then, the older man, the one who asked about the war, lowers his weapon to the ground and lays it at his feet before kicking it away. A few more follow suit, and then everyone has placed their weapon on the ground.

With them unarmed, I say, "Raise your hands in the air and go peacefully with our guards to the dungeon. The king will be down to speak to you about your surrender as soon as he can."

When several of the wolves scattered around the room shift and become men, the villagers gasp or shout, but none of them lower their hands.

I look away from the guards since they are all naked. I've never seen a naked man before, and I can't help the color that rises in my cheeks.

Besides, I have more important things to do. I rush over to the wolf that's been suffering all this time, the one lying in the foyer, and place my hands on him. Canaan tells me through the mind-link that he's going to go with the soldiers. I barely hear what he's saying as I concentrate on helping the wolf.

It's difficult and takes a bit of energy, but I'm able to heal him enough so that he can sit up. He thanks me with a nod, and then I hurry off to find the next person who needs my help.

I want to help everyone, but that won't be possible. I see Justin working on another wolf in the corner. He's in his human form, and thankfully, wearing clothes. "Bexley, there's another critical wolf in the library," he tells me.

I nod and rush down the hall. Ellison is there, also a human and wearing pants. He's pressing a rag against a wolf that's losing a lot of blood from an injury to his neck. "I've got it," I assure him, and he moves away. I press my hands to the wound, and my yellow light bathes the wolf so that the bleeding stops.

"How can I help, Bex?" Ellison asks.

"Uhm… I think it's called triage. Can you assess who is in most need of help? And don't we have nurses somewhere? The fighting is over. The women can come out of the vault. I bet some of them can help."

"Right." He rushes off, and I turn my attention to the wolf in front of me.

"You're going to be just fine," I whisper. He blinks at me a few times. I wish I knew who was who. not that it matters, but if I knew his name, I could use it to soothe him. I'm not sure the mind-link works with everyone, and I'm too afraid to try, so I just do my best to heal him and then move onto the next person.

We work tirelessly for hours trying to help everyone. The nurses come out of the vault to help, as well as Olive, Naomi, Anna, and some of the other women. Most of them have no medical training, but they can tie a tourniquet or place a bandage. The majority of the healing is done by Justin and myself, but no one else dies after the fighting ends.

Unfortunately, we'll be burying sixteen of our guards and twenty-three villagers, including Garth. It's a horrible loss for both sides, a tragedy that didn't have to happen, but thankfully it wasn't worse.

When Justin finds me in the library, still mending a broken arm, he says, "That's everyone, Bexley. We're all done. You did a terrific job. I don't know what I would've done without you."

I smile up with him and stifle a yawn. I think using this power must make me tired. I pat the warrior who has shifted into his human form, and put on pants, on his good arm and ask, "Where is Canaan?" Nervous anticipation bubbles up inside of me because I'm not sure if he can shift into his human form or if he'll be trapped as a wolf from now on.

Justin smiles, but I can't tell what it means. "He's waiting for you in the vault."

THAT FATEFUL NIGHT

I still don't know how to find the vault. Anna, who was standing nearby when Justin told me where to find Canaan, spoke up and said she'd escort me. Now, I walk with her up a back stairwell away from all of the blood and gore that the staff has already begun to clean up. As we walk, she tells me a story.

"It was the night of Prince Canaan's seventeenth birthday. King Paul and Queen Sophia wanted to throw a ball and invite all of the nobles from all the kingdoms near and far. Prince Canaan didn't want such an event, though. The king had just finished negotiating an agreement with the townsfolk for the villages between Luna Hollow and Hexeton to become part of the kingdom, and there had been some fighting. Canaan thought it disrespectful to have a party at such a time. His mother, who had a bit of a temper, decided if he wanted to act that way, she'd send all of the nobles home. They wouldn't celebrate at all. It was really a bit of a fit on her part, but he was fine with that because Canaan never liked to draw attention to himself anyway."

We climb the steps and I nod along, eager to hear more.

"Well, that night at dinner, there was a loud disturbance. The guards reported something large had landed on the upper walkway of the castle between the main turrets. They said it was a dragon. No one had ever seen such a thing. The king sent all of the guards to investigate, and then a woman appeared in the dining room. Dressed all in black with a green hue to her skin, she approached the king and asked him how dare he go against the treaty."

"That sounds terrifying," I say, holding my breath as she continues.

"Yes, it was. I was there. The king said he had no idea what she spoke of, but she insisted there was a treaty between the kingdom of Luna Hollow and Hexeton to always keep a buffer there so the wolf shifters wouldn't be able to invade the witches' territory. King Paul grew angry and asked her to leave. That's when she blew up in a rage and placed a curse on everyone inside of the castle." Anna shakes her head. It's clearly a difficult story for her to tell, and yet, it seems like she is gaining freedom from finally being able to share this with me.

"What happened next?"

"The curse was multilayered," she explains. "The king and queen both dropped to the floor, as still as death. Canaan attempted to shift so that he could protect his parents, but the witch cursed him as well. She said only if he could find his fated mate before his twenty-fifth birthday would the curse be broken. He must find her, and she must fall in love with him. She also said once she came here, if she were to ever leave, he would die. And no one who occupied the castle could ever leave for more than a few hours or they would die. Finally, if anyone ever spoke of the curse outside of the castle, it could never be lifted. Then, she was gone."

We've reached the top of the stairs and begin to navigate our way through the dark portion of the castle. "She did leave us a bit of her magic. Through trial and error, we found out about the letters magically appearing on the night of a girl's twenty-first birthday. Since all of the villages on the west side of the castle are occupied by wolf shifters, we assumed the girl would come from the east. We concentrated on the villages near Hexeton. And then, well, eventually, we found you."

"What about the memories?" I ask. "Why didn't anyone remember what happened to them here?"

"Also part of the curse. While it seemed impossible for us to be successful under the circumstances, parts of her curse helped us. We always did our best to hide the fact that we are wolf shifters anyway. It's long been a belief that humans aren't capable of seeing us as anything but a threat when they know the truth. I suppose that's true of witches as well. That's probably why most people in Hexeton don't realize they live amongst witches and are ruled by one."

"Queen Maeve is a witch?" I ask, surprised.

"She is indeed." Anna smiles and pats my hand. "As are you."

"But how? My mother isn't a witch. At least, I don't think she is."

"No, we don't think she is either. We believe your father must've been. We think the accident that claimed him in the forest that day was magic related, and that's why your mother won't speak about it anymore. Perhaps she'll be willing to explain it to you one day?"

"I hope so." I let out an exhausted sigh.

"We're almost there, dear," Anna assures me. "At any rate, you are here now. The curse is lifted—well, almost all of it. Canaan has one more task he'd like for you to do, if you are able. Then, we shall all have our happily ever after.'

"Happily ever after?" I repeat. It seems like something out of a fairy tale.

We turn the corner, and Anna stops walking. In the distance, I see a form standing in the shadows. "Good luck, dear," Anna whispers, and I step forward.

He's not twisted or hunched over, I can see that even in the dim light. He's not covered in fur and his hands don't have razor sharp claws. The closer I get, the better I can see him. His blond hair catches the light from one dim sconce a few feet behind him, and his hazel eyes twinkle, but they don't glow.

I stop a few inches in front of him and take him in. He's almost a foot taller than me with broad shoulders and muscular arms.

Through the fancy suit he wears, I can tell that his chest is chiseled and his abs are perfectly flat. That ache I've often felt low in my abdomen when I'm around him is back with a vengeance. I want to wrap my arms around his neck and kiss him with all the fire I have left inside of me.

But it's clear there's something troubling him. "Hello, Bexley," Canaan whispers.

His voice is less hoarse but still has a sexy rasp in it that makes my knees buckle slightly, especially when he says my name. "Hello, Canaan." I can't help but grin at him.

He reaches for both of my hands, and I give them to him. "This is me. This is what I looked like before the curse. Well, maybe a little younger, but basically the same."

"How does it feel?" I ask him.

"Incredible." He looks up at the ceiling and lets out an exasperated breath. "The moment I shifted into my wolf, I knew the curse was broken. I've only been happier at one moment in my life, and that happened right before then—when you said you love me."

I feel the heat rise in my cheeks. I distinctly remember that moment, too. I said it as I was blasting Garth across the room. "I do love you," I assure him.

"I love you, too. More than anything."

I can't stand it anymore. I push up on my tiptoes, like I did out in the forest, but this time when I press my mouth against his, I don't have to worry about fangs or his crooked mouth. He wraps his arms around me and lifts me off the ground, his tongue darting out to nudge my bottom lip. I happily open for him, and he deepens the kiss, sending those bolts of electricity racing through my body once more.

Eventually Canaan sets me back on the floor. The feel of his hand against my cheek is mesmerizing as he gently strokes my skin with his fingers. "What I said earlier, I meant. I want to spend the rest of my life with you. I want you to be my queen." He pauses, looking at me expectantly.

"Are you asking me to marry you?" I can't believe I'm even saying those words. Me? Marry the king?

"I will," he says, taking a bit of the air out of my sails. "But there's one more task I'd like for you to try if you're up for it before that. You see, I'd really love to share our happy moment with someone else."

Confused, I tip my head to the side. "Who?"

He clears his throat. "My parents."

ONE FINAL TASK

Canaan

The feel of Bexley's soft skin beneath my fingers has me wanting to forget about the rest of the world. I would love to pick her up, carry her back to my bedroom, and ravish her the way I've been dreaming of doing since the day we met.

But I have another important task for her. I'm begging the Moon Goddess that she'll be able to break the final portion of the curse and free my parents.

"I don't understand," Bexley says. "I thought your parents passed away the night the witch showed up?"

I know that Anna has told her the story of what happened that night. I asked her to do so as she walked with her to where we now stand. While it's true I probably should've done it myself, I wasn't sure I'd be able to. It's simply too painful for me to remember all the details. And Anna is an excellent storyteller.

"Ever since that night, they haven't moved," I explain. " They do appear to be dead, that's true. But they also haven't decayed, and when you broke the curse earlier, the others who were hiding in the vault said they heard each of them take a deep breath."

Bexley's nose wrinkles. "You had them hiding in a crypt?"

"No, it's not a crypt. We were afraid to place them in the mausoleum just in case they weren't dead."

"So… they're… where?" She turns her head to see I've left the secret door to the vault slightly ajar. "In there?"

I nod. "Yes."

"And you want me to… what? See if they're still alive?"

"Could you see if your yellow light does anything for them? While it might be a stretch, the fact that they seem to be breathing now and that the fated mate I've been waiting for for all of these years just happens to be a witch with healing powers can't be that much of a coincidence, can it?" I suck in a breath and hold it while she contemplates my statement.

It doesn't take him long. "Of course, I'll try," she says, putting a smile back on my face. "But please don't be disappointed in me if I can't do it."

"No, of course not, baby," I say, and she smiles when I call her that term of endearment. "I've been without them for almost eight years. It's been difficult, but all I'm asking you to do is try."

She nods, and I push open the door to the tomb. It's dark and cold here, but a few sconces light the way.

My parents still lie on the respective beds we built for them. Their hands are still folded on their abdomens, and they are perfectly still.

Except now, their chests are moving ever so slightly.

Hope wells up inside of me, but I try not to show my excitement as Bexley steps over to them and positions herself at my mother's feet. She extends her hands, and that soft yellow light illuminates the darkness.

I place my hands on her shoulders, hoping to pass my strength on to her, and she relaxes into my touch. A minute passes, then another, and nothing seems to be happening. Bexley shakes her head, but she doesn't give up.

And then… my mother's foot twitches. Bexley doesn't notice at first, but when Mother moves her leg, she sees it and gasps.

"That's it," I whisper in her ear. "You're doing it, baby."

Leaving one hand directed at my mother, she spreads her other over to my father. The more my mother moves, the stronger Bexley's powers become until we are all basking in a yellow light as bright as the sun at dawn.

My father lets out a groan, and my mother pushes up on her elbows. Bexley lowers her hands, and I rush over to help my mom as several of our friends rush into the room. Justin is at Father's side when he asks, "Wh-what happened?"

"Where are we?" Mother wants to know as I help her get seated.

"It was a curse," I explain. "Do you remember the witch?"

"Of course I do," Father says. "Where is she?"

"She's gone," I assure them, though it does bother me greatly that I have no idea where she went or if she might one day come back. "You've been unconscious for almost eight years."

"Eight years?" Mother shouts. "What?"

"We thought you were dead," David says with a jovial laugh.

Mother and Father look at one another and then at me. "How did you break the curse?" Father asks.

"I found my mate," I explain. "And she broke it." I gesture at Bexley, who has all but disappeared into the wall. She steps forward, and Naomi places a comforting hand on her shoulder.

"This is your mate?" my mother asks.

I suck in a breath. My mother and I haven't always gotten along, and if she says something negative about Bexley, I might just ask my mate to reverse the curse. "It is."

Mother stares at her for a long moment before smiling broadly. "Welcome to the family, dear." She opens her arms, and Bexley steps over, giving her a hug.

"What is your name, darling?" Father asks.

Once Mother has released her, she turns to him and says, "It's Bexley."

"Bexley?" he repeats, the same way I did when I first heard it. Then he laughs. "What a unique name."

Everyone chuckles, and then I make a profound statement. "Let's get out of this darkened vault and into the light. Everything is clearer when it's not enshrouded by shadows."

"We should have a celebration!" Olive proclaims as we step out into the hallway. Mother leans on my arm, and Ellison helps guide my father. "Is there champagne in the kitchen?"

"I'm sure we can find some," Anna says, and we all head downstairs to have a drink and celebrate the lifting of the curse.

The rest of the staff meets us in the kitchen. While I have sent the remaining guard back to their duties to protect everyone, we use the mind-link to invite all of the staff members and the rest of the household to help us celebrate.

We bust out the finest bottles of champagne, and everyone has a glass. Some people, like Ellison, have a couple of glasses. Despite having some stiff muscles and being a little groggy, my parents seem to be just fine, and everyone bursts into song, singing our traditional anthems.

Bexley doesn't know the words, but she smiles and claps her hands, even dancing a little. I can hardly take my hands off her, but when I realize Mother is beckoning me over to where she's sitting in the nook, I kiss the top of Bexley's head and cross the room.

Mother slips something small and round into my hand. "This was your great-grandmother's," she whispers. "I think it's time for you to have it."

"Thank you, Mother." She kisses my cheek, and I give her a hug. She has no idea what I've been through in her absence, and that story can wait for another day, but I have a feeling our relationship will be different after this.

I will also need to tell them that I am the king now, and everyone thinks they are dead. But that can also wait.

When the song ends, I motion for everyone to stop singing. "First of all," I say, "I'd like to take a moment to remember the warriors we lost tonight. Let us remember their souls as we celebrate our victory." I know my parents are lost, but someone will fill them in, I'm sure.

"May the Moon Goddess take them," Ellison says, which is our tradition. Everyone holding a glass raises it and drinks.

"Secondly, I have a bit of unfinished business I'd like to take care of right now." I clear my throat and cross the room to where Bexley is standing. She glances from side to side, like she's not sure what I'm doing.

"Bending down on one knee is easy now," I say as I do just that, "and I have you to thank for that, my love." Her cheeks turn pink, and she lifts her left hand to cover her mouth. "Nope. I'm gonna need that one," I tell her, and the crowd chuckles.

"What are you…." She gives me her hand and stops talking.

With her left hand in mine, I tell her what's on my heart. "Bexley, from the moment I met you, I knew you weren't an ordinary girl. I felt the tug on my heart immediately. But I was afraid. I didn't think a woman of your beauty, intelligence, and kindness could ever love a monster like me. But I was wrong. Your loving spirit allowed you to see past the beast and into my soul. Bexley Kessler, will you do me the honor of being my wife?" I slip the ring on her finger.

Bexley bursts into tears.

NOT A DREAM

BEXLEY

THE HAZEL EYES I SEE EVERY NIGHT IN MY DREAMS ARE STARING UP AT me, wide and hopeful, waiting patiently for me to respond to his question. A simple question. The most important question I'll ever be asked in my life.

This is not a dream. This is reality.

This is the real world—where people can turn into wolves, people can discover they have magical powers and use them for good, and people can come back from the dead—or like-dead.

It's a world where an ordinary girl like me can reluctantly move to a different kingdom only to discover she's been summoned to an enchanted castle to break a spell—and fall in love.

I'm struggling to answer Canaan's question not because I don't know the answer but because I'm crying so much. The only thing that could possibly make this moment more special would be if my mother were here.

She's not, though, and I can hardly wait to give him an answer, so rather than speaking, I nod my head fervently.

"Is that a yes?" he asks.

"That's a yes!" Ellison shouts from across the room on my behalf.

Canaan shoots to his feet, and his mouth clamps down on mine. I want to plunder his mouth right there in the middle of the kitchen, but I'm fully aware that we are not alone. The room explodes in applause, and then another song breaks out. Canaan spins me around in a circle, my legs flying out behind me such that I almost kick the kitchen island. Then he sets me back down. I have a feeling there's going to be a lot of random movement on his part for the next few weeks as he gets used to having his own body back and explores what it can do.

I am also excited to explore his old body.

He kisses me again, and over the sound of everyone singing and chatting, I hear his mother ask, "But what did he mean by 'see past the beast'?"

"We've got a lot to tell you," Anna says, and she's not wrong there.

I don't want it to be Canaan who has to stay and explain it to them, though. I'm exhausted, and I'm sure he is, too. All I want to do is go upstairs and climb into bed—and fall asleep in his arms.

"You're tired," he notices, running his fingers through my hair. I'll never get tired of the feel of his fingers. Before, he'd try to do that and couldn't, but now, his fingers slide through like my hair is made of spun silk.

"I'm so tired," I admit, managing to smile up at him. I still have my arms around his neck, even though it's a bit of a stretch for me to reach him.

"Let me say goodnight to my parents, and I'll walk you upstairs, all right?"

"Are you sure? It's been so long since you've seen them."

A crooked grin takes over his handsome face. "I'm sure."

That part of me deep in my core that always responds to him lights on fire. I have no idea if he will want to have sex tonight, but I suddenly don't feel as tired as I did before.

Canaan crosses the room to hug his mother and then his father. He pats Ellison and Justin on the shoulder and kisses Anna, Naomi, and Olive on the cheek. He also says goodnight to David and several other people I don't yet know as he makes his way back to me. Everyone waves at me, but they don't approach, and I'm fine with that. While I will one day be a part of their group, this is about the royal family, and I'm not that yet. Though, glancing down at the stunning diamond on my finger, I can't help but smile that I will be one of them very soon.

Canaan loops an arm around my waist and steers me out of the kitchen. I know he's tired, but he also has more energy than he has ever had before, since I've known him anyway. Seeing him this way makes me giggle.

"What's so funny?" he asks as we approach the stairs.

I quit laughing as I think of the bloody scene that unfolded here earlier. Thankfully, marble cleans up easily, and there's no sign of any of it.

Not even the spot where Garth's head came to a rest.

"I was just laughing at how much pep you have in your step now," I admit.

He chuckles, and I still love the sound of it, though it's slightly different than it was when he was a beast. "I'm so happy to be back in this form, I can't even tell you," he replies. "Tomorrow, Ellison, Justin and I are going to shift into our wolves and tear through the forest at top speed. It's going to be epic."

"Is that how wolf shifters have fun?" I ask him as we reach the top of the stairs and make our way down the hall. The blood is gone here, too. Some furniture and other pieces are missing from the hall, and the door to the parlor where Garth died is closed, but everything else looks normal.

"That's one of the ways we have fun." His tone is a bit huskier now, and a ripple shoots down my spine. "We have other ways."

I bite down on my bottom lip, flashes from my dreams flickering before my eyes. We reach my bedroom door, and I turn to face him. "Do you want to… spend the night with me?"

Canaan leans down and kisses me, his hands sinking down to my ass and lifting me up as his nimble fingers kneed my heated flesh. He tries to pull back, but I won't release him, my tongue darting out to keep hold of his. Eventually, I have to come up for air and find myself panting.

His voice is a low growl. "Does that answer your question?"

In response, I reach over and open my bedroom door, lacing my fingers through his and tugging him in behind me.

We lose our shoes on the way to the bed, his mouth devouring mine until he backs me into the mattress. With one hand, he yanks the blankets down, and then he starts to unbutton the row of buttons down the back of my dress. It doesn't take long for him to grow frustrated, and I hear a ripping sound.

I pull away from him and look over my shoulder to see the entire back of my dress has been ripped open.

Canaan shrugs. "It probably had blood on it anyway."

I shake my head, and he drops the fabric to the floor, leaving me standing in front of him in only my panties and bra.

"I see you're fully dressed," I murmur as his hands explore my lower back and my bottom. His laughter tickles my ear, his kisses heating the skin there. "Let's remedy that." I begin to unbutton his shirt, but once again, he rips it off, leaving us both laughing.

I reach for the button on his pants, and he says, "You aren't timid at all, baby. I expected you to be a little more lost."

I shrug and yank down his zipper. "I've done this many times." His eyebrows raise, and I add, "In my dreams. Don't worry—it's always with you."

"Well, okay then." He lowers his mouth back to my neck and sucks on the apex between my shoulder and throat for a moment, long enough to make my knees give out, before he raises his face again. "But how did you know what I looked like?"

I smile and trace a finger along his cheek, cupping his chin with my hand. "I knew."

It's answer enough for him. He lifts me up and dumps me on the bed, and I laugh while he sheds his pants and his underwear—and then I stop laughing.

God, he's gorgeous. My dreams were right—perfect pecs, washboard abs, and a cock I will struggle to manage but will do my best to consume.

He wraps his hand around the base of his dick and meets my gaze. "You sure about this, Bexley?"

Without faltering, I say, "Absolutely."

Grinning, he hooks his thumbs through my panties and yanks them off. The noise he makes when he takes me in, has my folds dripping in anticipation. His hand wanders up the inside of my thigh. I toss my head back and moan, longing to feel him inside me.

He plants a warm kiss on the inside of my leg, then my abdomen, as he climbs my body and rips my bra off without unhooking it. Then, he takes a nipple in his mouth and rolls it just like he does in my dreams. I thread my fingers through his hair and beg for more. His tongue slides up to my neck and then his lips are on mine, and I can't breathe.

The tip of his cock is poised right outside my entrance as I begin to rock back and forth, begging him to press inside me. Canaan lifts his head and looks into my eyes. "I love you, Bexley."

"I love you, too." I place my hand on the small of his back, pressing down to encourage him.

His smile widens. "So impatient."

I whimper and he taunts me by pressing in just the tiniest bit. I narrow my cycs at him. "Canaan?"

"Okay, okay." He kisses me again and moves in only slightly more. "This is going to hurt for a second, but then it'll feel unbelievable, I promise, baby."

I nod and spread my legs a bit further, lifting up to meet him because I really can't wait anymore. He pushes in and twists his hips a bit. My mouth drops open as the feeling of being stretched overwhelms me, but it doesn't really hurt at all, and then, he's kissing me again, and our bodies begin to move as one, just like in my dreams.

It doesn't take long at all before I am completely lost to the world. I tip my head back and let out a moan, sinking my fingers into his back, and Canaan's mouth clamps down on my neck again. This time, he's not sucking though. I feel his teeth pierce my skin and let out a little yelp.

"Sorry, baby." His breath fans over my ear, the side of my face, and where my neck stings. He kisses the spot a few times, and the pain fades.

I couldn't possibly pay attention to anything else anyway when he begins to grind against me, hitting me in just the right spot. I cry out again, my abdomen contracting a few times, nearly lifting me off the bed. If he wasn't on top of me, I might curl into a ball. "You're so close," he whispers. "Come on, Bexley. Come for me."

At his command, my body gives in, and I begin to spasm around his cock. My mouth drops open, and I can't breathe or think. All I can do is revel in the euphoric feeling that rolls over me.

Seconds later, Canaan begins to move a bit faster. He grunts a few times and then buries his head in my shoulder before groaning. His body jerks a few times, and I feel his warmth spread between my legs.

My lungs burn as I suck in air, wrapping an arm around him and feeling my body dissolve into the mattress. He rolls off me but keeps his chest pressed to my side, one arm draped protectively across my stomach. "Are you okay?"

I turn to look into his hazel eyes. "I've never been better." I mean it.

He smiles and kisses me, and I roll into his chest. Canaan pulls the covers over us, and I reach for sleep, praying that this hasn't all been a dream and that when I wake up in the morning, he'll still be here in his human form. I fell in love with a beast, but this is the man that will be my husband, my king, and his love is the most beautiful magic of all.

EPILOGUE

Bexley

Six Months Later...

Mother is weeping.

It's nothing new. She does a lot of that these days. Ever since the day after the castle was attacked when Canaan and I showed up at the house she shared with Harvey and told her everything, she's been teary-eyed. She's so proud of me. Even now, she says, "I can't believe you're the queen!"

"Well, not yet," I remind her, looking at my own reflection in the mirror. "There is the matter of getting married—and coronated."

"That's all just a technicality," she assures me. "I'm so proud of you, honey!"

"I'm proud of you, too." Carefully, I turn in my long white dress and hug her. The last thing I need to do is tear this gown, though I'm fairly certain Canaan will do that later when he grows impatient with all the buttons.

"Leaving Harvey wasn't easy, but I know I made the right decision," she says. It had always been clear to me that Harvey wanted a second housekeeper, not a wife, and when he tried to treat Canaan the same way he'd treated Garth, like he was a means to an end where Harvey would benefit, I pointed it out to her. Now, she lives at the castle with us, and she and Sophia are fast friends.

Even though no one outside of the castle knows that the king and queen are still alive. They'll be at the wedding today incognito, and then, they'll retire to a family estate in the far western reaches of Luna Hollow where Sophia has already made me promise we will bring our litter of grandkids at least ten times each year.

We haven't started on that litter yet, but we do enjoy practicing for when the time is right.

"It's almost time," Naomi says, poking her head in the door. She'll be my matron-of-honor, and Fiona and Olive, who is temporarily back in town from her own kingdom just for the wedding, will serve as my bridesmaids. Canaan will have Ellison, Justin, and David, who cried when he was asked, standing beside him.

Best of all, Anna will preside over the ceremony. Apparently, she is also an ordained priestess! I swear that woman can do anything.

Mother reaches up and smooths back my veil. "Are you ready, dear?"

"Absolutely," I tell her, and we both laugh. Locking arms, we head out into the hallway that leads to the main part of the temple. I'm still learning a lot about the Moon Goddess and the wolf shifters' religion, but I'm happy to have the ceremonies today take place in this sacred place that is so special to Canaan and his family.

The organist begins to play, and Naomi heads up the aisle first, followed by Olive and Fiona, who keeps giggling every time she makes eye contact with Ellison. She's not twenty-one yet, but I do hope as soon as she has her birthday she realizes he's her mate. I would love to have my other best friend live in the castle with me.

I see Olive wave at her mate, Rex, whom she met when she was finally able to go home after the curse was lifted.

But then, Mother takes my arm and starts to move me into the temple proper and up the aisle, and my eyes meet Canaan's, and I can barely breathe. He looks unbelievably handsome standing there in his royal regalia, a deep blue suit with a sash, his crown catching the lights above us.

I'm not sure what Anna says when I arrive in front of her. Mother kisses my cheek, and Canaan takes my free hand while Naomi takes my bouquet. All I can do is look into his eyes and think about how far we've come.

I go through the motions, repeating after Anna, bowing to receive my crown as queen, swearing allegiance to the people of the kingdom and to protect them always, even saying the vows I prepared. If I got them right or not, I'll never know because all of my concentration is on him.

When it's Canaan's turn to say his vows, his eyes glisten with tears. He keeps it simple. "Bexley, when I first met you, you didn't believe in magic at all. It turns out, all the magic you ever needed was locked inside you. When you opened your heart to me, you let all of that magic, all of that kindness and love, out into the world. You change everyone you meet for the better. I will forever be changed because of your love, and for that, I will be eternally grateful. I will also protect you, love you, and cherish you until my dying breath."

By the time he's finished, tears are streaming down my face. He reaches up and brushes them away with his perfectly formed human fingers, and I can unequivocally swear I do believe in magic.

Anna gives him permission to kiss me. Canaan wraps an arm around my waist, tips me backward in a low dip, which has the crowd oohing and ahhing, and then sets me up to capture my mouth with his.

When he releases me, with the crowd cheering, he whispers in my ear, "Come on, baby. Let's go make some magic." I take his hand and let him lead me out of the temple ready for whatever adventure comes next.

From now on, the only place Canaan is allowed to be a beast is in the bedroom, and I'm okay with that.

Thank you for reading! Book 2 will be out soon. You won't want to miss the wolf shifter take on Sleeping Beauty!

ALSO BY BELLA MOONDRAGON

The Alpha King's Breeder series:

Bought by the Alpha: The Alpha King's Breeder Book 1

Loved by the Alpha: The Alpha King's Breeder Book 2

Lost by the Alpha: The Alpha King's Breeder Book 3

Luna of the Alpha: The Alpha King's Breeder Book 4

Legacy of the Alpha: The Alpha Kings's Breeder Book 5

Daughter of the Alpha: The Alpha King's Breeder Book 6

Descendants of the Alpha: The Alpha King's Breeder Book 7

Shadow of the Alpha: The Alpha King's Breeder Book 8

Son of the Alpha: The Alpha King's Breeder Book 9

Spare of the Alpha: The Alpha King's Breeder Book 10

Claimed by the Alpha: The Alpha King's Breeder Book 11

Atonement for the Alpha King: The Alpha King's Breeder Book 12

Rejected by the Alpha: The Alpha King's Breeder Book 13

Abducted by the Alpha: The Alpha King's Breeder Book 14

Wolf Shifter Fairy Tale Retellings series

Beauty and the Alpha Beast

Sleeping Beasty

Tangling With the Alpha

The Luna's Vampire Prince series:

The Culling

The Kingdom

The Conquered

Pregnant With Four Alphas' Babies

Chosen As the Breeder

Mated to Four Alphas

Threats Against the Breeder

At War for the Breeder

The Stolen Breeder

Four Alphas, Four Babies

Becoming the Luna Queen

Descendants of the Breeder

Desired by the Devil series

Whispers of the Devil

Banter of the Devil

Murmurs of the Devil

The Mafia Kings series

Indebted to the Mafia King

<u>Loved by the Mafia King</u>

Claimed by the Mafia King

Secrets of the Mafia King

Burned by the Mafia King

Kidnapped by the Mafia King (coming soon!)

Dark Stalker Romance series

Tempted by Sin

Fated to Sin

Secret Billionaires series

Finding the Secret Billionaire by Olivia Bhelle Kildare

Falling for My Secret Billionaire by Bella Moondragon

Driven by the Secret Billionaire by ID Johnson

Wolf Shifter Alpha Kings series

Ravens and Ruins

Sundrops and Shadows

Snowflakes and Sabotage

The Vampire King's Feeder series

Claiming the Alpha's Daughter

Loving the Alpha's Daughter

Finding the Alpha's Daughter

Bewitching the Alpha's Son (coming soon!)

Writing as B. Moon

The Boy Who Died

Sign up for Bella's newsletter here.

*Or get a free novella from The Alpha King's Breeder series when you sign up here:
The Beta and the Maid*

Follow Bella on Facebook here.

Follow Bella on Bookbub here.